MW00509263

A native from Lorman, Mississippi and the middle child of five siblings raised by a single mother, Jamie has been married for the past sixteen years and writing for the last ten.

She's a private person who loves travelling and writing about different places with her own uninhibited twist.

Jamie Phillips

PRIMAL DESIRES

The Hunt Begins

AUSTIN MACAULEY PUBLISHERS™

LONDON • CAMBRIDGE • NEW YORK • SHARJAH

Copyright © Jamie Phillips (2018)

The right of Jamie Phillips to be identified as author of this work has been asserted by her in accordance with section 77 and 78 of the Copyright, Designs and Patents Act 1988.

All rights reserved. No part of this publication may be reproduced, stored in a retrieval system, or transmitted in any form or by any means, electronic, mechanical, photocopying, recording, or otherwise, without the prior permission of the publishers.

Any person who commits any unauthorized act in relation to this publication may be liable to criminal prosecution and civil claims for damages.

A CIP catalogue record for this title is available from the British Library.

ISBN 9781788231831 (Paperback)
ISBN 9781788231848 (E-Book)
www.austinmacauley.com

First Published (2018)
Austin Macauley Publishers Ltd.
25 Canada Square
Canary Wharf
London
E14 5LQ

Acknowledgements

I want to start off by thanking God. Because without him, I wouldn't be here. Next, I want to thank all those who said I wouldn't make it. Because of you, I strive harder.

Now, my family. The best way to describe them is 'open minded and uninhibited'. My true and always loyal fans. My sisters and brother, especially. You've given me so much and I thank God every day for giving me the best siblings in the world.

To my husband the unexpected adventures, the unique experiences, and your uncanny wild side is why I'm writing today. Thank you. I love you and appreciate you.

My uncles. My mom's brothers. One isn't with us anymore, physically, but the love I feel for him in my heart is still the same. Watching my uncles as I grew up was the most amazing thing in my young life, especially my mom's younger brother.

I remember when I was around ten or eleven when he was in a very bad accident. He was young, still living in my grandparents' house. I remember the women calling and coming by to see him. One even bought him a big color TV with a remote control (that was the shit in the early eighties). So, I stopped watching the women and started paying attention to my uncles.

I learned it was their charm and how they carried themselves with that die-hard country boy style; how they would get up five days a week to make a living and never complain about it. Then watching them transform from rugged country boys to southern gentlemen. They will forever be in my heart.

More thanks to my best friend who is more of a sister to me than a friend. You are the realist person I know. Our conversation keeps me on the right track; even when I didn't know I was wandering off the straight line.

Mom, you've had some hard times. But I hope the accomplishments your children and grandchildren have made and are trying to make will give you something to look forward to in the future. A single mother who raised five kids. All of them made it out of high school and three graduated from college. One graduated Cum-Lau and the other got her masters. Grab you a platinum, relax a little bit and glorify in the fact that you did a damn good job. Luv u mom.

And to the publishers and editors of this book. Your patience is amazing. To have an author like me to join your family means so much to me; I can't begin to put into words. Thank you.

This is a work of fiction. Any references or similarities to actual events, real people, living or dead, or to real locales are intended to give the novel a sense of reality. Any similarity in other names, characters, places, and incidents is entirely coincidental.

I apologize about the name change of the series, but it had to be done. What you once knew as '*Animal Instincts: The Hunt*', is now '*Primal Desires: The Hunt Begins.*' The first book of this series. For those of you who haven't read the first book, you can go to www.amazon.com to find my books. You can also find it on Kindle.

I hope you enjoy reading '*The Hunt Begins,*' as much as I enjoyed writing it. And thank you so much for reading my books. Be on the lookout for my second novel in the '*Primal Desires*' series titled: '*Primal Desires: Mating Season,*' coming soon.

—Jamie

Preface

"Motif! It's happening!"

As I sat in the corner of my mother's suite, praying the shadows would hide me from this horrific scene, her screams almost made me piss my pants! And my father was nowhere in the room.

Just me. Tatum.

The son of an asshole who just so happens to be the Chief of Gerillian Island. Being one of the oldest islands miles away from the Brazilian mainland, known as 'The Hidden Treasure Island', Motif De' Amadre believed in the ancient laws and lived by them, which is why, just minutes ago, he had his personal assistant bent over her desk. I ran to get him after my mother's nursemaid Noonie, yelled at me and pushed me out the door, when my mother doubled over screaming. Since he was busy, I decided to leave a note, wanting my mom to stay home and have the baby here. Motif was ecstatic about the ritual, but my mom would get this sad look on her face and soon, would cry. My father would yell at her and make snide remarks about her status in the community.

My mother Ky Flask, daughter of Elder Vilmander Flask and Mistress of Geri Island, is legendary for being the first mate to ever live through a 'Birthing Ritual'.

"We must prepare you for the ceremony."

Good, that bitch Noonie was already in there.

Though Noonie is my mother's maid and supposed to take care of all of her needs, I didn't think those needs included my father. One day, my mother sent me to get him from his chambers to take a family portrait. When I entered through his sitting room, I didn't think his bedroom door would be open (he never leaves his bedroom door open), but it was, and so was Noonie. She was on her knees in front of my father, with her head buried between his legs. It's also the first time I caught him cheating on my mom. He didn't see me because his eyes were rolled into the back of his head.

"Aaahh! Noonie, please get Chief Motif for me. I don't think I'm going to make it this time. And send my son to me please."

For weeks, the coming of the new baby was all the people of Geri talked about. The traditional birthing was the main rule the Chief's wife had to follow. When I asked my father or mother what they had to do at the ceremony, their words to me was always, 'not yet, but soon.' My father always said it with a smile on his face, but my mother...I don't know... it was different.

Like it was fear or something.

"Your mother wants to see you," Noonie said with a smug smile on her ugly ass face, as she strolled to the double mahogany doors.

Bitch.

As I entered my mother's bedroom, the scent of cinnamon invaded my nostrils. It fit her perfectly. Cinnamon skin tone with long sleek black hair, and hazel eyes like my own. She was sitting on her chaise when I approached. She had on a flowing white silk gown that betrayed her huge milk filled breasts and bulging middle. Her smooth skin seemed waxen today and her long hair was in a loose knot on the top of her head. It was terrifying to see pain on my mother's face and the fear in her eyes was agonizing.

"Tatum, come. I need to feel the embrace of my sweetest spice," she said as her usual greeting to me. I ran as fast as I could across the large spacious room and into her waiting arms. "Tatum, your father and I are going to go bring your new baby brother into this world. I have known you for four years and it already seems like a life time. As you know I am the first to live through a 'Birthing Ritual' but this time might be different. I feel that your mind is wise enough to grasp what I'm saying.

"Tatum, I believe you can master anything in this world. I know it bothers you that people always telling you that you're too little to do big things. But even little people make the world go round. I want you to take care of your little brother and raise him to be as you will become," she said with tears in her eyes. It hurt so much, I couldn't do anything but hug her tighter, wishing I was big enough to stop what was about to happen.

"Ky love!" my father yelled from the sitting room. He marched into the room taking long strides and took my mother from my embrace. "We have to get to the

13

ceremony before the baby arrives." I knew how much he wanted another son to grow and marry a Chief's daughter from a neighboring tribe. Something my mother was not happy about. She wanted her children to make their own decisions in the future. But my father said we must stick with tradition.

"I'm ready. Tatum, remember what I said, I love you," she said kissing my tear streaked face.

"Stay in the palace and obey Noonie," my father said rushing her to the door. And then they were gone.

~~~

Screams from down the hall woke me out of a strange dream. One I do not want to remember. I looked on my nightstand and saw it was 2:58 a.m. I crawled out of bed and tiptoed down the hall where the shouting was coming from.

My father's chambers.

It sounded like the other voice was Noonie's. I made sure the guards were not in sight as I kneeled and peeped through his keyhole. I couldn't see her face, but it was obvious she was upset because my father was in my view sight and he didn't look upset at all.

"See, I told you this would happen. You should have married me instead. Because she was able to live through the first birthing didn't mean she could do it again. Now look, I'm stuck raising kids that should have been mine in the first place!"

As I look through the keyhole, I noticed the groin area of my father's silk robe that matched my mother's was covered in blood down to his knees. "Noonie, if you value your life, you'll watch what you say about my wife. And if you ever mistreat my kids, I'll stick your head in the wolves' cage while you're alive." From the tone of his voice I knew he was serious. "And don't tell Tatum his mother died. I'll tell him myself. It's best he knows now that women are replaceable wives."

"Motif, what are you saying exactly?" Her voice changed. I leaned closer making sure not to bump into anything and giving myself away.

I watched as my father moved away from my view, removing his robe at the same time.

"I'm saying I want you to be my wife Noonie. If you're stuck raising my kids and sucking my dick, I might as well make you my wife."

I rose from the door and made my journey back to my room with thoughts of my mother and vowed right then and there that I would do as she asked. Whatever I do in this life, I won't stop until it became a mastered skill. Even if it meant becoming a better man than my father.

Chapter One

Nine years later...

My brother and I sat patiently waiting for the elders and our father to start this so called 'necessary meeting.' I watched the panel closely with a straight face, learning a long time ago not to show emotion in public. A trait my father had failed at.

"Well, I don't know where to begin," Motif said nervously. A first for him, I think.

Since the night I eavesdropped on my father's conversation with Noonie, I found different ways for my brother and me to keep our distance from them. We were never in the same room with them for more than five minutes before I had an excuse for us to leave. Sitting this close to him now was claustrophobic.

"I don't mean to speak out of terms here, father, but Boaz and I have to get going. I promised I would teach him how to feed the wolves. Then we're going to meet Karden at the courtyard library."

"Patience, son, is a virtue."

Bullshit! I know he's not trying to be a father now. The only time he ever spoke about patience is when he told Noonie that they had to wait the appropriate time after my mother's death to marry.

"The Elders and I have called you here today to discuss your futures."

Shock and fear ranged in my head like church bells bouncing off the wall. I knew the time would come when my father would speak of the arranged marriages, but not this soon. I'm only thirteen, for Christ's sake!

Probably, just my imagination.

"We want to talk to you about your future wives."

Holy shit!

"Boaz, you are too young to understand what I'm talking about right now, but you, Tatum, are ready to train your pack and future mate."

It is tradition that the eldest son of the Chief starts training his servants which is called the 'Wolf Pack.' Born to protect the way of nature. The Pack consists of seven young boys of native blood who learn different fighting skills and will grow to become strong young men who produce male heirs to continue the tradition. The future wife would be of the same age as the young Chief in training and must have a trace of 'Indian Warrior Heritage Blood.' But that is not supposed to happen until the young boy reaches the age of sixteen.

"Excuse me, but do you realize I'm only thirteen?"

"Yes Tatum, but your mind seems to be older than your age."

Well, at least he got that part of it right. I'm a straight A student who has already moved up five levels past kids my own age and fluent in four different languages and working on the fifth. My father was not pleased that the people of Geri think I'm a special spirit who will make for a superb Chief. Ten times better than Motif.

"We think you are ready son." I think he saw the hesitation in my face because he added, "Do it for me." That comment alone would have made me storm out of the meeting, dragging Boaz with me. But that would mean a separation from my brother if I decided to wait until I was sixteen. That meant Boaz would have to marry someone who would not be of his choice and he would forever be under our father's and Noonie's demanding hands.

I learned that my father planned for Boaz to marry Noonie's cousin whose father is Chief of a neighboring tribe— one my father wants control over. So now I have the choice of starting my own pack, and I'll be able to save my brother ↓ if I can play this meeting to my advantage.

"Okay father, I'll do it as long as Boaz can train with me." I knew he would not agree, but he could not stop what the elders agree to.

Boaz started bouncing in the seat next to me. "Please father, please. I won't get in Tatum's way and I'll be extra quiet. Please!"

"Son, I don't think that's a good idea. I have other plans for you. You shouldn't be so attached to your older brother because the separation will be harder. You should spend time with your mother."

I took my cue.

"Which would you rather have, father? Boaz spending time with me, learning the ways of a Chief, or with Noonie, learning the ways of a woman?"

He looked as if his head was about to blow off.

The elder who was sitting next to him, Elder Nuieve, stood and placed his hand on my father's shoulder. "He is right Motif. We are raising strong young boys to become men, not women. To him, it is just fun. Though I am quite sure he's just as brilliant as his talented brother."

"You're right. It's not good to have a young boy under his mother so much."

She's not his mother! But father was agreeing, so I kept my mouth shut.

"Now let's get to work. We have found several young boys who would be of a value to your pack."

Best to start putting my foot down now. "No offense father, but I would like to choose candidates for my pack myself."

Motif looked as if he wanted to jump across the room and slap me across the face for speaking out of turn. Before he could voice his anger, the eldest of the council, Elder Calese stood and gave the final word. (It was no secret that the council detests confrontations and long meetings).

"I agree with young Tatum. How would we know if his wise mind would make for a good Chief of this land? Young Tatum, the Council will give you a month to prepare your candidates and present them before us. As for your chosen mate, that too is also yours to choose."

My father was steaming mad. He wanted me to marry the Keekulo's daughter. Their tribe is right off the mountains. It is said jewels are embedded in their rocks.

"What!? Noonie and I have already found a mate-"

"Noonie is not my mother and since she's not, that arrangement is void."

That did it.

He started his long strides across the room to slap my face, but once again he was interrupted by the council leader.

"He's right. Your wife is not his biological mother. Tatum, we will allow you to find your own mate. If you do not succeed in one month, or if the girl chooses not to be your bride, then the arranged marriage will go on. Is this agreement understood?"

I didn't want to look a gifted horse in the mouth, nor did I want to stay and hear the tongue lashing my father was sure to give as soon as the Council cleared the room. It's better to leave now while the room is still full.

"Yes sir. May we be excused now? I would like to get started as soon as possible."

"That's a good idea. The Council needs to meet with your father alone. If you have any questions, don't be afraid to ask. And Tatum, remember when choosing your pack that you follow the way of the traditional word."

I nodded then lead my little brother out into the baking Brazilian sun.

Chapter Two

My list was already made. I began working on my candidates the same day of the so-called 'necessary meeting' and the choices were easy. I chose my best friend, Karden, as my right hand man. Even though our intellects differed, he followed the tradition to a tee. Next was my brother because he was my shadow and would do anything to protect me like I would him. The rest were Pierce, Moham, Cole, and Tyvine, −all sons of the Council. The hardest part was finding a mate. I met Karden at the library courtyard and told him what I planned.

"So you are going to go to North America for a girl?" he asked, stunned.

"Not just any girl, this one will be able to live through the 'Birthing Ritual'."

A while back, Karden and I stumbled across a passage in the old law book about some sick shit that, without a doubt, made me queasy to my stomach just thinking about it. But if my research is right, the ritual will be the last thing on my mind. My actual plan is to get my brother far away from Motif, but the only way I can do that is to become Chief...

"But she will not be from a neighboring land."

"The traditional law clearly states that the chosen female should have a tribal native lineage, but it didn't say she had to come from a specific area."

"Okay, but why North American?" he asked, still looking confused.

"Remember we had to do that history report last fall on destroyed tribes from different places?

"Well, in America there were several native tribes that were destroyed by people who settled in their region. Some of the tribal women were raped and killed, and those that got away, went into hiding. The children of those women in this day and age have mixed blood.

"But there was this one particular tribe called the Chickasaws. The entire tribe was known as powerful warriors. Even the women trained with their men. Their job was to protect the tribe while the men went to battle. The tribe was ambushed, and most of the women were raped and killed. The rest escaped and migrated to different areas of the world. But I'm focused on a small area. A state called Louisiana."

"Okay, I'll bite. Why Louisiana?"

"Once I found out how our mothers died, I figure no woman can take that kind of pain and survive. But studies and reports done show that certain women have survived worse. I knew that women here cannot take that kind of pain and live to see the next day. From birth to adulthood, these women are treated as fragile. Too damn delicate to touch, and too damn close to home. I need someone strong.

"This girl in particular has mixed blood. She's part Choctaw, Chickasaw, and African heritage. Several of her ancestors were raped and many died but her linage can be traced back. Her linage was traced all the way to Milwaukee and ends in Louisiana where she is located."

"Tatum, do you hear yourself? The girl you are looking for could be black. Your father will kill you!"

"The traditional laws only state tribal linage, not what color her skin has to be."

"Well, since I'm part of your pack now, I guess I can't question your decision, but tell me why America at all?"

"Haven't you heard anything I said? To my father it's about how much land he can rule over and who all he can control. He was jealous of my mother because she survived my birth and the people adored her. The law did not say that if there was a second pregnancy that she had to go through the 'Birthing Ritual' again. She could have had my brother safely at the hospital. She would have been alive to raise me and Boaz.

"For me, after the traditional birthing, my wife will live to raise our child. I want my mate to have the same background of a warrior, someone who will mirror my image. Not someone who can wax my dick just to make me feel like a man," I said in anger.

"How are we supposed to get there?"

"My Uncle Demarcus. By him being an Elder on the Council, my father won't question him."

"Okay, that's figured out, but how are you going to get the parents of a thirteen-year-old girl to let you take their daughter away?"

"Good question."

Chapter Three

I awoke to the pilot's voice over the intercom asking us to fasten our seat belts as we landed. My Uncle Demarcus was with me and my pack. He told my father that he was taking the Pack on an educational vacation before they started their training. My Uncle was more like a father to me than my own was.

When it was announced that Cole (his only son) would be a part of my pack, he approached me and laid a hand on my shoulder and said with tears in his eyes, 'I wouldn't have it any other way. You boys are brothers now.' I knew how much he despised my father. Hell, who didn't? Motif felt he could have whatever he wanted and what he wanted most was more land and more pussy.

"Wait here boys. I had arranged for a car to pick us up from the jet once we landed."

No sooner had he spoken the words than a shiny black Lincoln Navigator pulled up. As we loaded up in the truck, Uncle Demarcus was telling our little group what he had planned.

"I got us rooms at a small hotel in- what was the name of that town again, Tatum?"

"Houma, Uncle Demarcus. Houma, Louisiana."

After driving for two hours, the houses turned into shacks spaced very far apart, sitting on high wooden legs. The vegetation here was stuffy. If I rolled down the window and reached my hand out, I probably could touch every leaf we passed by.

"I think we're lost. The first store I see, I'm stopping to get directions."

I won't argue with that. This place looks like a big green maze.

We saw a shack up ahead with several vehicles parked in front of it (mostly pick-up trucks). It had May's Café on top.

"Come on boys and get yourselves something cold to drink, while Tatum and I get directions."

Uncle Demarcus couldn't speak English too good, so it was obvious that I would have to do all of the talking.

As soon as we entered, all eyes were on us. Even though we had on jeans and t-shirts, our long black hair and cinnamon skin tone stuck out like a sore thumb.

A chubby woman behind the counter greeted us. "Welcome to May's Café," she said in a deep, thick accent. "What can I get ya?"

Uncle Demarcus looked at me and I spoke.

"Could we please be seated at a table? And my brothers and I would like lemon ice tea please."

The woman looked surprised. I guess my accent startled her.

"Honey, you can have a seat anywhere. I'll be right out with your drinks."

I spoke in our native tongue to my Uncle and everyone in the room quieted. I lead us to a table that could seat four people, then told my brothers to move another table closer and to bring the chairs.

One of the locals, who was clearly not shy, asked, "Where you people be from?"

"Mind your business Jack, and leave these folks be," the chubby white woman said. "Now what else can I get ya?"

She put the drinks on the table, eyeing my Uncle. He was thirty-five years old and had wide shoulders and trim waist like the rest of our fathers have.

"Do you know where Patricia Ann Beau lives?" I asked.

She looked as if she would have run out of here just from the mention of the woman's name.

"What you know 'bout Pat Ann?" she said in a stern voice. "That old traiteur woman has evil on her land. If you want to live to see tomorrow, its best you stay away from that old woman and that evil child she's raising."

"Why do you think she's evil?"

The woman pulled up a chair and sat beside me at the table. My brothers looked confused, so I told them in our native tongue that I would explain later. Karden and Boaz knew how to speak English, so their expressions made the pack wary.

"Thirteen years ago, Pat Ann had a daughter name Ella T, who was pregnant by a man she did not know the name of. As soon as she gave birth, that fast ass gal ran off and left the child with Pat Ann. We, as Cajuns, stick

27

together 'round here, so us women gathered up supplies that Pat Ann would need to raise the little one. She was more than happy when we showed up with all that stuff and invited us all in for some gumbo as a thank you. I member my ma, May Sue had asked to see the child. I member it like yesterday," she said with a faraway look in her pale eyes.

"Pat Ann led us upstairs to the child's room and as soon as she swung that door open, we all hauled ass trying to get as far away from that place as possible. The baby had bronze color skin with silky wavy black hair, and long lashes. We Cajun's don't show fault to what color your skin is and we don't now, so don't get it wrong. We ran because the baby was asleep with a large black python snake curled around her little body. We thought for sure that the snake had killed the babe, but the next day Pat Ann came to town with the child in her arms and the child was holding a coral snake in her small dimpled hands.

"Never seen anything like it," she said, shaking her head.

"I would hear stories from some of the people who'd been ill that went to Pat Ann over the years to be treated and they always say, that girl always sits by the pond playing with water moccasins and things of the sort."

"Do you know where she lives? Have they moved?" I asked anxiously. I don't know why, but instead of me running with my tail between my legs, the story just made me want her more, and I haven't even seen her yet.

"Boy, ain't you heard what I said? The girl is evil!" She looked around the table and saw no fear on our faces.

"Well, it's your life. Go two miles down the road and make a left at the first opening ya see. Then make a right and you'll be at her house. Ya best to get going now before night falls so you won't drive off in the water."

At those words, I stood and my Uncle and brothers did the same. He took a hundred dollar bill and gave it to the lady. She rose to get his change and I told her to keep it. She gave me the stunned look again.

"It's for the information also."

She smiled and waved as we walked out. "If ya need anything, just come by here and ask for May Belle and I'll come runnin'."

As we all piled back in the car, I gave Uncle Demarcus the directions and told them what May Belle said.

"Tatum, do you think this is a good idea? She's one of them and even they think she's evil."

"I don't think so. My gut is telling me she's the one."

"Tatum...I know that you are very wise for your age but something about this doesn't feel right to me."

"Put it this way Uncle, if she is not for me there is always the marriage my father arranged for me."

"Humph."

It was hitting below the belt, but I knew if I mention something my father decided on, Uncle Demarcus would do everything in his power to help me.

Ten minutes later, a small shack on toothpick legs was before us. It was a cute, little shack that looked as if it was supposed to be in a fairytale. It was painted white, with red trimming and rose vines climbing the sides and front of the house. The front porch was screened in, so you were able to enjoy the fresh air without the pesky bugs. A small pond was visible in the back with a little boat tied to the dock. Suddenly, an old woman with a picnic basket full of vegetables in her hand came from the woods that surrounded the shack. When she saw our car, she stopped and I could've sworn she was looking directly at me, even though the windows were tinted dark. She approached the porch, sat her basket down and waited as we descended the truck. The heat was excruciating, but it didn't seem to bother her none. As I got closer, I could see the wrinkle lines in her pale white skin and—

What the fuck! It looked as if she was aging more before my very eyes.

Her eyes fell on me.

"Well, it took you long enough to get here. Did you have a safe flight?" the old woman said, pulling me into her embrace.

Okay, I was lost. "I'm sorry Miss, but I think you have me confused for someone else," I said, easing out of her arms.

She tilted her head to the side. "You mean you're not here to get Jameria, my granddaughter?"

I moved away from the woman and closer to my brothers.

She laughed. "Don't be afraid. Come and let me explain."

Chapter Four

The woman opened the screen door and led us inside. Cole, Pierce, and Moham stayed on the porch while my Uncle, Karden, Boaz, and I took seats at the small kitchen table.

"My name is Pat Ann," the old woman said with a smile. She went to the refrigerator and started pulling ingredients from it. She laid a big batch of shrimp on the kitchen table and place two bowls on each side.

"If you don't mind, could you start peeling the shrimp for me? Jameria would do it, but I asked her to pick some wild strawberries for the cheesecake we're having for dessert. Since she's the only one who's not afraid of the snakes and there are snake pits everywhere near the berries."

As we started to hull the shrimp, the old woman explained.

"Jameria is not like any other person around here or in this world, as far as I know. People here are afraid of her, for no damn reason. Because a child can get along with nature so well does not make them evil, but in the beginning I had my doubts.

"Snakes would lay on my porch steps as if they were waiting for her. When she turned six, the poisonous snakes would keep their distance from her. One day, I was down by the pond pulling in some fish when a water moccasin was right there by my feet. Jameria was in the house doing her lesson—the children at school was frightened of her as well, so I took her out of school and now she's being home schooled. But anyway, I must have been gone for a long time because she came out to check on me.

"As she approached, the snake moved out of his striking position and quickly escaped to the water. Two pythons, the size of gators, slithered in past her and into the water. She asked, 'Grandma, did it hurt you?' I didn't even know she saw the thing from so far away. She didn't wait for my response either.

"I watched as she kicked off her shoes and dove into the water with her clothes on. She was under water for so long, I thought I would have to get the police to search for her body. I was about to run in the house to use the phone when the two pythons emerged and Jameria followed behind with the water moccasin in her hand. She said in the sweetest voice I've ever heard in all my years on earth, 'Grandma, is this the one that tried to take you from me?'

"The snake was still alive in her small hand. Over the years, I had become accustomed to Jameria's strange gift, but this one was the strangest. She was only six, you see, and I was already too old to teach her. That was my first time seeing her swim and also seeing a poisonous snake in her hands.

"I stood bobbing my head up and down, not knowing how to move my tongue after watching what was going on before my very own eyes. Then, just as casually as she asked her question, she tossed the thing to the pythons. One of them swallowed it whole, while the other made its way back to the yard. She said, 'Don't worry Grandma. I won't let anything take you away from me.'"

"I realized at that very moment that my beautiful granddaughter would have to leave this place before something bad happens," she said wiping her hands on her apron. She came to the table and grabbed the bowl of shrimp and dumped them in the sink.

"How did you know I was coming for her?"

She had her back to us as she prepared dinner. "Faith."

"Huh?"

She turned around and looked at me with a big grin on her face.

"I prayed that one day soon, someone would come and offer me relief. I'm an old woman and Jameria is only thirteen years old. Once I'm gone, there will be no one here she can go to. Her good for nothing ma had ran off with some fool on a motorcycle. Her father, who's part Houma Indian and African American, left as soon as my daughter said she was pregnant. He hasn't been back since."

She went to a small closet and pulled out a metal bucket, dumping the hulls from the shrimp in it and placing the bowls in the sink. "You guys can wash up right here. I'm going to take these out back and dump them."

My little brother jumped up.

"I'll do it for you, Miss Pat Ann," he said in English. I knew the only reason he wanted to take it was because the pond had ducks in it.

"Well that's mighty nice of you lil one. What was your name again?" she asked, putting her hands on her hips.

"Boaz."

"Aahh. You have a biblical name. Well Boaz, sure you can, but be careful that you don't go too far from the house." Then she showed him to the door.

"Now where were we? Oh, yeah, how did I know? Your eyes are like hers. Both of you carry the same determined glint. It's all over your face and the way you walk, which makes me afraid for anyone who crosses you. You are also a leader. I noticed the way the young boys follow your command without even asking why. But Jameria, on the other hand, may not understand because she is not a follower. She's also a leader. Those snakes—"

Screams broke the old woman's revelation.

It was Boaz.

My brothers and I ran out back. Boaz was lying on his side sliding back and away from the pond. Directly in front of him, three snakes in striking positions was about to attack him. A menacing hiss from behind us rang so loud and clear that even the snakes with the rattles on their tails, stopped rattling.

34

Two extremely large snakes were on each side of our group. Suddenly, a bronze skinned girl with honey brown eyes and long wavy hair came through the back door of the shack. She ran and crouched protectively in front of my brother. The two snakes that were closer to us slithered right up next to her. She had no fear in her eyes. Her hair hung over her face and shoulders like a shield. Her thin t-shirt and tight jeans revealed long muscular limbs. There was definitely some warrior linage in her blood.

"I don't care if he isn't family," she said in a sugary sweet voice. "You know the rules."

At that, the two pythons attacked, striking fast like lightning. Each of her snakes was about five feet long. One was the color of silver, with green shapes crisscrossed on its back, and the other was canary yellow with patches of white. After their meal, they glided straight into the water.

Everyone around, including myself, stood shocked in place with our mouths hanging open. The girl stood and turn toward us. Her lovely face held the expression of anger.

"Grandma, what happened? Why did you let him go near the pond?"

I could tell she was trying her best not to show real anger towards her grandmother. I also understood why the old woman would want her granddaughter to be taken care of after her death. People not liking her, would take advantage of a sweet girl like her.

She looked down at my brother. "Are you alright? Were you bitten?" She knelt beside him, looking for wounds.

My brother stared at her with fascination in his eyes. "No. How did you do that? I've never seen anything like that in my life," he said laughing.

She smiled, her face revealing her soft side. But just as quickly as it came, it was gone. She wasn't angry anymore, but she dropped the smile. I guess from all the ridicule of being called evil, she kept her distance from strangers.

"I don't know," she said quietly. She stood then reached out a hand to help him up. He introduced himself in English.

"Portuguese?" she asked.

It must have impressed my Uncle, but it was nothing to Karden and me. We'd gotten used to being smarter than our years, so her question wasn't surprising to us.

"How did you know we speak Portuguese? Have you been to the country?"

"Well sir, that depends. Do I get an introduction if I answer your question?"

Uncle Demarcus couldn't help but smile at her charming way of letting us know we were being rude.

"My English isn't so great. But my nephew would be more than happy," he said, pointing me out.

Our eyes met for the first time. I thought I saw surprise in hers for an instant, but I could be wrong. I approached her, offering my hand in greeting.

"Hello, my name is Tatum De'Amadre. You've met my little brother Boaz, and the rest are Pierce Kemp,

36

Moham Shiller, Karden Poteece and Tyvine Seal," I said pointing to each of them. "And this is Cole and Demarcus Flask."

She shook my Uncle's hand. "To answer your question, Mr. Flask, I don't want to seem sarcastic, but the answer is simple. I read. And...I also speak a few words," she said in our native tongue. My Uncle froze looking from me to her.

"Come. Let's go inside for some supper. You boys can go and wash up in the kitchen. If anyone needs to use the bathroom, it's on the left down the hall," Pat Ann yelled back to us.

As I walked beside Jameria, the scent of brown sugar and strawberries invaded my nostrils.

"So, what brought you guys here?" she asked, being conversational.

Before I had a chance to answer, her grandmother said, "We'll talk about it inside."

Chapter Five

The kitchen table could only seat four people. So Tyvine, Pierce, Boaz, and Moham ate in the kitchen. Karden, Cole, and I ate on the porch gallery with Jameria, Miss Pat Ann, and Uncle Demarcus. We ate a bowl of soup with all kinds of sea food in it that she called, "Gumbo," and a square piece of cornbread. Boy, it was delicious.

"Jameria," her grandmother began, turning so she could look her straight in the eyes. "We have never been the type to beat around the bush about what we have to say and I'm not about to start now."

The old woman took a deep breath. "These people are here to take you back with them and I think you should go."

Jameria looked as if her grandmother had lost her mind. "What?"

"Look, this young boy is in an arranged marriage and this is his only chance to make his own choice. You of all people know how it feels when other people make decisions for you, before you have the chance to choose.

"He's from a wealthy tribal island, one of the rarest today. Now before you start with the questions, I had already asked if you chose not to marry him at the age of twenty-one, you both would be free to make your own decisions. If he chooses someone else, he would send you anywhere you want to go with your own little fortune."

She realized the old woman wasn't playing.

"Grandma, you want me to leave?" She was hurt. Tears streamed down her pretty face.

"Honey child, now you know I don't want you to leave," she said pulling the girl into her frail arms. "I'm old, Jameria. My numbered days have turned to hours now. It took me so long to get from the garden today that I had to ask these young boys to shell the shrimp for me."

"That's why I need to stay grandma. So I can take care of you," she said against the woman's shoulder.

"No, Jameria, that's why you have to leave. If I died tomorrow, no one will be there to take you in and help you finish your schooling. The Lord has sent us a blessing and I think you should do it. I know that you are smarter than your peers but these people here won't be fair to you and that frightens me."

She looked up. "I'm not afraid. I can take care of myself."

"I'm not afraid for you. I'm afraid for them. The first person tries to take advantage of you will pay dearly, and I will not have my only granddaughter chased down by some angry mob."

The girl dropped her head in defeat. "How long do I have?"

"Tonight."

She looked up again, surprised. "Why so soon?"

That's when I spoke up. "Our Council will meet with us in twenty-six days to see if I've chosen the right candidates for my Pack."

"Your Pack?" she asked, arching her eyebrows.

"Yes. The group of boys with us is my Pack. I'm to be Chief of our Island one day and it is important that the training starts at an early age."

"What kind of training and why do you call them 'The Pack'?" she asked, clearly interested.

"Any type of combat training your body and mind can master, of course, and the actual name is 'The Wolf Pack'; born to protect the way of nature."

I don't know what it was I said, but her whole body language changed and her eyes locked onto mine in a mind blowing conversation, one only we could understand. I was confused and intrigued at the same time. They were telling *me* to come closer with a blind spot on everyone else. I wondered if anyone else noticed.

Without a word, her grandmother started carrying the dishes inside and my brothers and uncle decided to help. Was that a coincidence or did she really make that shit happen? I explain to Jameria the rules of our tribe, trying to ignore her silent call.

"There are five main rules we must follow: Each member of the pack's wives must go through the 'Birthing Ritual.'" (I decided to get that one out of the way first, since it was the hardest to explain). "But we have a long time to worry about that. The second is to never harm the wolves. They are known to our people as the sacred animal. If one pack member fights, we all

40

fight. The third one is, never disrespect the Chief's mate. The consequences could be deadly. And the last and most important rule: The Chief has the final word."

I held her gaze, wondering what was going on in her head.

"Why me?" she asked.

That was easy. "The laws of our people states that the chosen mate had to be of native tribal lineage. You have four different types of lineage in your blood."

"I'm not the smartest person in the world, but I have read some of the Brazilian laws, and I haven't come across anything that sounds halfway like what you are saying."

I got up to sit beside her, and the brown sugar scent of her skin hit me again. Was it *my* choice or did she make me sit next to her? It didn't matter, because whenever I was close to her, I felt different.

Complete, somehow.

"That's because we have our own island close to the Brazilian mainland. How do you know so much about it anyway?"

She looked at me as if I had asked the most ignorant question.

"The snakes. Brazil has several different types of snakes in its region, but it's only one I'm interested in. Anaconda."

I knew exactly what she was talking about. I hurried and changed the subject, because the thing terrified me.

"I need to know that you agree to leave with us tonight. I really would like you to come."

She stood up and left the gallery, walking around the house to the pond. I followed, figuring since I was with her, the predators that glided the ground wouldn't hurt me.

"I'll have to leave with you tonight?"

"Yes," I said from some distance behind her.

She knelt and placed her arm (elbow deep) in the water. Then she stood and backed up a couple of paces. She took a couple of steps to the right, placing her body directly in front of me. I didn't see it at first because I didn't think to look down, but the huge yellow and white snake was in front of her.

"I'm leaving tonight and I will never return." The snake moved toward her and wrapped its body around hers. It wasn't attacking but caressing. "I need you to protect grandma here until her final days are over. I love you friend and I pray you never forget me as I won't you."

The snake made a hissing sound.

"I'll take Coral with me. Bye, friend."

The large snake slithered off of her thin frame and went into the water. She turned and I saw tears in her eyes, but they still showed no fear, only sadness. It hurt me to my heart to know I'm the cause of her feeling this way. I hate feeling selfish!

"Jameria look, you love this place and I don't want you to—"

"Grandma laid it all down for you, didn't she?"

"Huh?"

"The people here hate me and I've done nothing to them. But she's right. The day she dies, they will probably come after me for no reason and I will defend myself. Even if it means taking a life...I have no choice."

Before we left Brazil, I went on the internet to find out the legal way for Jameria to return home with us. But it seems all of that was wasted.

While Jameria was in her room packing, her grandmother had some documents on the kitchen table in front of Uncle Demarcus.

"I don't let Jameria come into town with me when I go shopping for the things I can't grow. Too dangerous for her. I had the passport done a year ago and the adoption papers four years ago."

Everyone stared at her.

"Four years ago, a man came to my house for medicine. Jameria was sitting on the floor reading. The man waited until I went in the back before he rushed to pick her up and run out of the door with her. I didn't have to chase him."

She didn't say another word. She didn't have to. We all knew those snakes didn't let him get a hundred yards out before they attacked his ass.

"In this country, we are not allowed to let a child leave without a parent or guardian." She lean down and signed some papers, then laid the pen in front of my Uncle. "You will have to be her guardian. I don't have to tell you not to mistreat her. You've seen firsthand what will happen."

He looked at me nervously. I nodded. I didn't have to think twice. I wanted her like I needed air to breathe.

He picked up the pen to sign, then gave her the copy and placed the original in his breast pocket jacket. Jameria came from the hall carrying a black duffel bag. I nodded to Moham, who took the bag from her.

"It's best we get going. The sun has already sat," my Uncle said standing.

The old woman grabbed my arm as I was about to go out of the door. "You take good care of my honey child, and remember your promise if she chooses not to marry you."

I nodded and walked out of the door.

Ten minutes later, after we were all seated, Jameria came out with tears in her eyes and a red and black snake wrapped around her left arm .Uncle Demarcus was about to protest when he realized it was coming with us, until I looked at him and shook my head. That little snake was nothing compared to what else she could have brought.

Chapter Six

Jameria was not allowed to stay in the hotel in Houma, so my Uncle decided to drive us back to the airport. He said that once we get back to the mainland we would stay a night there, then boat home. Jameria's traveling outfit was a dark pair of jeans that flared at the leg with a white t-shirt and black and white running shoes to match. She told me that her grandma never had much money and it didn't bother her, but at times the UPS man would show up with something her grandmother had ordered for her.

"We're taking a private jet?" she asked as we approached the air field.

It was Karden who answered with glee. "Actually only the Chief and his mate have full access to the planes. We were given permission to take this on an educational trip."

She looked confused but didn't press the issue.

Once we boarded the plane, Uncle Demarcus pulled me to the side.

"What do you plan to do with her until Council meets?"

"Since we have to train in the View House, I was thinking she could stay there."

He nodded. "You'll have to dress her in appropriate attire."

"We'll take her to the dress shops on the mainland tomorrow."

Boaz was sitting beside Jameria holding her snake. He seemed just as comfortable with it as she was. I took the seat on her other side, next to the window.

"What will happen to me if Council decides I'm not the right candidate?" she asked. I guess she was probably making plans for herself if things don't go the way *we* planned.

"The final word falls upon me."

It was late when we made it back to the mainland. As Uncle Demarcus said, we stayed a night at a hotel. Jameria had a room all to herself. She said it was the first time she'd ever stayed in one. I couldn't wait to see her face when she saw the palace.

The next morning, we took her shopping. The dressmaker took her size, and told her that she would make her many dresses in many different styles. Since Jameria wasn't fluent in our language yet, I translated for her. We bought her several outfits and different types of jewelry to match. She tried on a white silk bikini top with matching silk pants that complimented her bronzed colored skin. I had Uncle Demarcus buy her a diamond link belly chain. She let her long thick hair hang down all the way to her waist, with leather sandals that had strings crisscrossed up her muscular calves, but you couldn't tell from the silk pants.

After Jameria's little shopping spree, (she hadn't seen the big one yet), we had lunch, then took the boat back to the Island.

"You have your own yacht too?" she said, impressed.

As we approached the Island, my brothers gathered around to watch the expression on her face. From a distance it looked as if the entire palace was rising from the water. The large beige stucco had several wings jutting out from the main building in different directions with hundreds of long windows. The vegetation around the palace was thick, creating a paradise feel.

Her mouth dropped open. "I've never seen anything so beautiful in my life!"

"You better start getting used to this beauty if you're to become the Mistress here," Moham said, grinning.

"Who's the Mistress now?"

"No one. Our last Mistress died nine years ago. The Chief remarried, but that's just a marriage of convenience." It was Karden who answered that time. He knew how much I despised my father, so he decided to provide a nice way of saying, 'Noonie ain't shit'.

When we docked, my brothers took her things to the View House. She had a white silk hooded cloak, that I helped her put on.

"I want you to keep your head covered until we're inside. We will stay in the View House while we train and if you need anything, The Pack will answer your call."

"What's my call?" she asked, covering her head.

I let out a bark that even made me jump.

"Oh, I don't think I can do that," she said, shaking her head.

"Don't worry about it right now. They will be close by, since we have to prepare for the meeting."

She didn't bother looking around, because she knew I wanted her to remain inconspicuous.

I lead her straight to the View House. It was the eastern wing closer to the docks, with six columns covered in green vines. The double oak doors were already open. She stood in the doorway, staring at the ceiling to floor rows of books.

"This is where we will be staying for the next twenty-four days. While we are here, you will learn the rules and the laws of this land. I speak four different languages as you will also learn. I want you to be fluent in our language before the Council meets too."

We walked to the end of the long hall. There were two doors, one on the left and one on the right, covered in dark blue satin material. I opened the one on the left and let her enter first. The room was decked in bronze and beige satin material. It was something I had done before we left for North America. I wanted her stay here to be as comfortable as possible, or until she moved into the palace.

"This will be your room." My brothers were there putting some of her things away. "Normally your maid is supposed to do this type of thing for you, but we can't take the chance of having you exposed yet."

She nodded her understanding. Once they were done, they all filed out, bowing to her as they passed.

"Umm... Could you not do that? You don't have to bow to me," she said shyly.

"Yes we do," Cole said. "Whether you want to believe it or not, we already consider you our Mistress. You'll just have to get used to it."

She turned to me. "They're not staying?"

"No. There are only two rooms in here. One for the Chief and the other for the future wife. The Pack will keep us informed of anything important that we will need to know."

"So since your people know that you are back, do they know I'm in here?"

"Yes, but no one is allowed to see you until after the meeting. No one but The Pack, that is."

"Will they drill The Pack about who I am?"

Instantly, Boaz popped into my head. She knew something was wrong.

"What?"

I started toward the door. "Nothing I can't handle." I opened the door a little and barked The Pack call.

Perfect. Exactly who I wanted to hear. Cole's lanky limbs came charging back to the door. I opened it wider to let him in and closed it quickly.

"Cole, I need you and Karden to go get Boaz, and keep him with you until this thing is over."

I knew he wanted to ask me, 'What will my father say?' but Pack rules are not to question the Chief's order. I'm sure Karden will explain it to him.

Jameria walked up beside me with the snake wrapped around her arm, licking her face.

Cole looked from me to her with a strange expression on his face. It wasn't anger, so I didn't ask any questions. He bowed to us, before he turned and left. I locked the door behind him. The last thing I needed was for one of my father's women come walking in here. There were rumors about him taking many women to bed all over the palace.

"Am I not allowed to ask you any questions either?" Jameria said, pulling a book from the shelf.

I had to laugh at that one. "The rules are The Pack is not allowed to question the Chief, but I think that is going to be kind of hard for you to master."

I got my first genuine smile from her today.

While we were shopping, she didn't seem all that interested in the clothing, which pleased me. She was not materialistic.

"I need to do something and from the looks of things, I don't think it's any way for me to avoid doing it at night."

"What is it?"

She placed the book back on the shelf and took a seat in one of the leather bound chairs. "I need to take a dive in the water, to let my presence be known."

This must have something to do with the snakes. "I don't think that's a good—"

"I know it's your job to protect the wolves, so you should know where I'm coming from," she said with a firm jaw.

She was right. After what I witnessed back on her homeland, I knew she'd go without my permission.

50

"We'll go to the docks tonight after everybody is asleep. You should go prepare for dinner. Put on anything, since we are going out later."

She laid her snake on the table. "Stay right here Coral. I'll bring your dinner when I'm done."

Okay, that's going to take some getting used to.

After my brothers left that night, Jameria and I sat down and had a long talk. I told her about my accomplishments and everything else I wanted to master. She told me about her goals she wanted to pursue in life.

She introduced me to her snake Coral, by letting it lick my face.

"That's his way of getting to know you."

She took one of the mice from a cage she purchased on the mainland and sat him on the table in front of the snake. Before the rodent made it halfway across the table, Coral slithered forward and swallowed him whole. Later that night, we snuck out the side door that was closest to the dock. She whispered something to the snake, then let it go on the ground.

"Let's go. He'll let us know if someone is coming."

How the hell does she do that?

At the dock, she took off her running shoes, jogging pants, and sweater, revealing a black bikini top with a matching thong bottom. Her muscular thin frame was beautiful to look at. Too beautiful, I might add. She dove in the water and I stood watching, making sure the coast was clear. It seemed like a long time, but she finally emerged. I knelt down and grabbed her hand, pulling her

51

up. When I turned to get her clothes, I saw something red at the other end of the dock.

"Is that a sign?" I asked.

She looked over my shoulder and saw the snake curled up.

"Yes. Come on."

I grabbed her clothes and she grabbed the snake as we ran back through the side door, just as my father's guards came around the corner, heading toward the docks.

Chapter Seven

For the past month, my Pack and I wrote down different skills of combat that we would like to train in. They came early in the morning and would leave late in the evenings. Jameria took a great interest in this one. Never before in our history had a woman ever trained with The Pack, nor was there a rule against it. So my future mate will train with me personally; there won't be any questions asked.

I gave The Pack the weekend off to relax and used that time with Jameria, teaching her our native language. I was glad to know she's a fast learner. It didn't take her any time to catch on. We spent every moment together. At night, I would let her crawl into my bed with her snake and we would play a game called, 'guess what language is being spoken.' To my surprise, she could speak Ancient Latin. That started a whole new language for me to learn. I decided if I need to speak to her without everybody knowing what I was saying, (including The Pack), this would be the language, though it might take years for me to learn it.

Jameria became my best friend and I hers, in just a few short days. She told me that she never had friends other than her snakes and her grandma. Two weeks after Jameria arrived, Uncle Demarcus sent a letter to her by Cole. It was a telegram letting her know her grandmother had passed away in her sleep. (I hired a home health nurse to check on her every day). She locked herself in her room the entire day, only allowing me to enter. The only time I left her alone was when I told The Pack to go relax for the rest of that day. She snuggled up close and laid her head on my bare chest and cried herself to sleep that night.

The night before we were to meet with Council, Uncle Demarcus came to give us a head's up.

"Your father thinks you haven't found a mate yet, so he is going to present his case tomorrow. He wants to have Noonie present."

"Why?"

"I don't know, but I hope you two are ready," he said eyeing Jameria also. "He's probably going to try to use your age for not making the right decisions."

Motif would do anything to get what he wants. And right now he wanted land more than he wanted me to be happy. I told Jameria everything about my father. She despised people who take pride in exploiting their children.

I told my uncle we had everything under control and not to worry. But from the expression on his face, that's all he'll be doing tonight.

~~~

My Pack and I waited until they sent for us to present the new pack members. My brothers and I were dressed in nothing but black silk loose fitting pants, with our hair down. Jameria wore a black satin dress that stopped at her bare feet, with ties around her neck and slits up her thighs. The bodice was skin tight showing her thin muscular frame. When she walked, the satin material flowed behind her like wings, showing off her long smooth bronze legs that could go on for days. Her hair hung down to her waist in black waves. She had a black satin cloak to match, to keep her concealed until I was ready to present her.

Knock. Knock. Knock.

Jameria stood and turned her back to the door, placing the hood of her cloak over her head. I opened the door and looked up at my father's guard.

"The Council will see you now," he said in a deep rustic voice.

We filed out of the house into the heat, but the breeze from the ocean was pleasant. As we entered the chambers, my group broke into formation—keeping my mate and me at center point. We broke again and became a straight line with us still in the middle. The Council stared at us with unspoken awe on their faces.

They were impressed.

My father was staring at the hooded person next to me. I could see the wonder written all over his face.

"Young Tatum, we can see you were successful in your hunt. We all thought it would be impossible for you to take on such a healthy task," Elder Nuieve said. "Even your father had doubts."

I looked at my father and Noonie sitting beside the panel looking puzzled. I turned my attention back to the Elders.

"Present your pack."

Each member introduced themselves, saving Jameria for last. When her time came, she stepped forward and untied her cloak, letting it fall to the floor around her bared feet. There were gasps from everyone in the room except for my Uncle and The Pack. I don't know if the shock was because of her stunning beauty or the fact that she was a young lady of color.

Jameria held her head high and began to speak. "My name is Jameria Rena Beau—"

"What is the meaning of this? This girl is not from this land or any other land around here," my father said with his face masked in anger.

I stopped the Elder before he started to speak by holding up my right hand.

"She's of native blood. Actually, she's of four different types of tribal lines." I nodded to Karden who was on my right, took some papers that were tucked under his arm and gave one to each council member.

When he returned, I continued. "By our laws, she has the right to stand as my mate."

Elder Nuieve stared at her. "It says here, your ancestors were tribal warriors in North America. Do you speak our native language fluently?"

"Yes."

Noonie, realizing what was about to happen, whispered something in Motif's ear.

"Elder Nuieve, this girl does not have a wealthy background. You cannot allow such a thing."

"The laws do not speak of wealth or how much money the chosen mate should have," I said, a little smug. He cut his eyes at me with the slapping look in them again.

"Elder," Noonie began. "There is no way for me to raise this, this...this girl," she said with distaste.

I was getting real irritated with her ass. "Noonie, you are absolutely right. You cannot raise anyone above you. The mate of the Chief in training can only be raised by her father."

I waited for it, wanting the shock to hit her in the face.

She smiled and said, "By law, she cannot remain here. Her father is not here to claim her."

My smug smile turned into a flat out grin. Uncle Demarcus's face mirrored my own as he stood and made his way to the podium.

"I lay claim to Jameria Beau, as my daughter. I have her legal adoption papers right here," he said, revealing the documents.

"Which means Jameria is legally the Mistress of Gerillian Island," I said looking directly at Motif.

It wasn't the Elders who stopped my father from kicking my ass this time. Before he took two steps off the podium, Jameria was in front of me in a defensive crouch with each of my brothers taking her flanks. I was protected in the middle of the V formation. A menacing hiss came from her lips, making my father take a step back. The panel stood, taking a few steps back of their own, when a snake, that's well on its way to becoming the next anaconda, slithered up beside her. It had black sparkling scales and deep green eyes that shined like emeralds.

The entire time, my pack never broke rank. As if it was expected.

So I acted like I expected it too.

"No matter how you feel about her, she is my choice and that's my final word."

Elder Nuieve decided to speak, after a long deliberation. "The young lady is definitely of warrior blood. You have my blessing, Young Tatum." Each member gave their blessing, while my father stood dumbstruck.

He couldn't say shit. His eyes were glued to Jameria's snake.

"Now that we have resolved that issue, I don't feel it necessary to have the snake present," Elder Nuieve said.

Jameria didn't move. Her eyes were locked on my father, daring him with her eyes to make a move. I stepped forward, placing my hand on her shoulder. Over the past month, I understood her not trusting people, and this was one of those times.

"It's okay."

She leaned forward and whispered something to the snake, and he was gone. She stood out of her defensive pose and my pack followed suit, stepping back into the straight line we were in when we first entered the building.

"I must admit Young Tatum, this is some female you have found, and I'm really impressed with your pack.

But I thought you would've picked someone else other than your brother. Your father had plans for him. Plus he's younger than the rest of the boys."

I looked over at my little brother, standing beside Jameria. I did something I knew my father would never do.

"It's Boaz's choice."

Boaz glanced at me, surprised. He's normally afraid of our father, but today there was no fear in his hazel eyes.

"I want to be in Tatum's Pack." He looked up at my father and spoke in a language only our pack could understand. It was French. He was reciting the traditional code of honor: "Our lifespan is from earth, so we will protect earth and all living things in it."

Noonie's mouth fell open, knowing this wasn't something that she'd taught him. Jameria taught Boaz French while she was learning Portuguese.

It looked as if my father wanted to say something, but he took one look at Jameria and decided against it.

"I don't think in all of our history have we found a group so attuned to each other. I think this will be the strongest 'Wolf Pack' we will ever have," Elder Shamar said.

Motif was so upset. I could see his nostrils flaring from here.

"There will be a bonfire tonight, to greet the new Pack," Uncle Demarcus said. He looked at each of us. "Enjoy tonight Pack, because your training begins in two days. It's going to be a long time before you can have fun again."

59

Later that night, Jameria came out of her room dressed in a purple silk and chiffon skirt that touched her ankles, with slits up the front of her thighs. She had on a purple bikini top with ties around her neck and her hair loose. The only jewelry that adorned her body was the diamond belly chain around her waist and the coral snake wrapped around her arm. I had on purple satin loose fitting pants, to match her outfit with my hair also loose.

Since this was a celebration night, my pack was already down by the beach.

"You ready?" I asked. She nodded handing the snake to me. She didn't like leaving it alone, so I told her I would carry him with us.

The rumors were already circulating before the Council Meeting was over, about my chosen mate. I'm sure the beach will be full of people from all over the palace and neighboring Islands.

I let Coral wrap around my right arm and took Jameria's hand as we departed.

When we made it to the beach, it was just as I thought.

It was crowded.

We made our way down the beach and everyone turned to get a good look at the new Mistress of Geri Island.

I spotted my brothers sitting at a long table a few yards away, and made my way there, dragging Jameria with me. Elder Mara stopped us on our way.

"Young Tatum," he said with a slight bow. He eyed the snake wrapped around my arm and took an automatic step back. "Is it real?" he asked.

I smiled and held my arm up so he could get a better look. When I brought it closer to my face, Coral licked my cheek. Several people, who were close by, held the same expression Elder Mara had. Bottom jaw hanging, with bulging eyes.

"Well," he said struggling to find the right words. "I would like for you and your mate to meet a few people."

He walked around introducing us to different people of wealth. My father and Noonie were sitting with the Chief of the Keekulo's, when we came upon their table.

"Chief Tykanae," Elder Mara began. "I would like to introduce you to young Tatum, son of Motif. And the lovely young lady beside him, his future mate, Jameria."

Chief Tykanae looked over at my father, then back at me. Not once did he acknowledge Jameria.

And that shit pissed me off.

He extended his hand to me in greeting. "There is always time to change mates," he said.

I raised my hand to grasp his and Coral hissed at him. He pulled his hand back immediately.

"I've already made my decision," I said looking at each one of them.

"Tatum," my father said to me with a slight shake in his voice. With a snake wrapped around my arm, he tried to play nice. "You shouldn't have—"

I walked away, pulling Jameria by the hand. "Come on. I want to get something to eat." Since they couldn't treat my mate with respect, then whatever he had to say to me, he can say it to my back.

Motif stood, coming around the table.

"I've had enough of your attitude!"

You would think he learned his lesson at the Council Meeting, but I guess it's true; that old saying about you can't teach an old dog new tricks.

Just like earlier today, Jameria crouched in front of me. The hissing sound, coming from deep within her, could be heard all over the beach. My brothers heard it and came charging down the beach, taking the V formation stance with me protected once again. If my father wanted to get at me, he'd have to go through Jameria first.

Motif looked around him at all of the faces here.

I did too.

They stared at Jameria with the expression of wonder and admiration on their faces.

I saw the jealousy in my father's eyes immediately.

He took strides toward her. "I will not let this girl dictate me being a parent to my son."

He was inches away when the black snake from earlier today was on the right side of us, and a green snake with gold stripes, that just join the party, glided to our left. The snakes curved around our little group in the shape of a heart, separating us from them.

"He may be *just* your son," Jameria began, addressing him for the first time.

"But to me he's more. He's my Chief, my Pack leader, my mate, and most of all… my friend." She stood and raised her head high. "I will not dictate how you raise your son, but I will not let you threaten him, or let you do anything physically harmful to him either."

Motif glanced from me to Jameria with astonishment in his eyes.

I don't know how my face looked, but my heart was beating so fast, I thought it was going to beat out of my chest. And it had nothing to do with the scene going on in front of me. It was Jameria in her aggressive pose. It was something about the way she moved that sent my heart into over drive. I didn't know what all that meant but there was one thing I knew for sure. Motif and Noonie were going to have to start respecting Jameria as their Mistress. This outcast shit was going to end tonight.

Jameria backed up, grasping my right hand. Coral uncurled from around my arm and slithered up hers and into her hair. I turned and addressed my father.

"Her name is Jameria or Mistress. If you cannot address her when you see her, then I suggest you go another way and never cross her path. She is your new Mistress now. It's best that you, Noonie and anybody else who visit this island treat her as such."

Jameria hissed and the snakes broke rank, gliding back into the water. My brothers stood and formed a straight line, with three on each side of us. She held her other hand out to Boaz. He took it and Coral glided out of her hair and down her arm to Boaz's. It curled comfortably around his slender arm. My pack and I left my father and his company standing there with their mouths hanging open.

Chapter Eight

Three years later…

Our first hunt was around the corner, and my pack was prepared. For the past three years, we trained in different martial arts skills. From kickboxing to jiujutsu, our pack was the best trained group of warriors ever in our history. All thanks to my mate.

After we moved into the palace, we started each morning off with weapon training and our nights ended in our studies. Jameria became fluent in six different languages. The tutors from the mainland said that her I.Q. level was off the charts. By next year, she will be attending college with me. I was already a freshman taking online courses. Our plan was to attend Harvard together in the fall.

During the afternoons, my brothers and I would do chores around the palace while Jameria studied the traditional law. We were in the barn grooming the horses when she walked in, obviously annoyed about something. I assumed it was probably something about Noonie again. Lately Noonie had been trying to spend time with her, but just the sight of her irritated Jameria so bad that she would spend the entire day in the snake pit, if I don't go get her. (Only I was allowed to enter the pit).

"Tatum, I need to talk to you," she said using the Latin tongue. Whenever she uses *that* tongue, my brothers would walk away knowing she didn't want them to hear.

"What is it?" I asked in the same tongue. I was cleaning the mud from one of the horse's shoes.

Jameria was never the type to beat around the bush about what she had on her mind, and she wasn't about to start now.

"Why didn't you explain the 'Birthing Ritual' to my grandmother before you brought me here?"

I dropped the pick and looked up. She was fuming mad and I was speechless.

It didn't matter. She'd already started to walk away.

I called my brothers so they could finish up in the barn, while I went after her.

She was already across the yard, headed towards her palace wing.

I walked slowly up the stairs and knocked on the double wood oak doors. She didn't answer, so I let myself in.

She was nowhere in the room but her closet doors were open in her bedroom. I peeped around the door and saw her with her old duffel bag thrown over her shoe table, stuffing whatever she put her hands on, in the bag.

"What are you doing?" I said, coming farther into the room.

"Leaving."

"Why?" I knew the question was dumb, before I asked.

She spoke in the Latin language again. "Because the only reason I'm here is to birth your baby, then die. Every time I asked you about your mother's death, you changed the subject. You even told The Pack not to tell me!"

I stared at her as she spoke. I hadn't noticed how much her body had changed. She'd already developed a woman's figure with high full breasts that jutted out the little blue silk triangles of her bikini. The curve of her hips and her small muscular waist could put a super model to shame.

Damn!

I always considered Jameria as mine since the day I went to get her. So her leaving wasn't an option. Her being my friend was the added bonus, but the dreams were my punishment. My dick would rise right before I dosed off to sleep with her in my arms. Every dream had her starring in sexual fantasies that a porn star would die for. But this wasn't a dream.

To lose her would kill me, or cause me to kill myself.

I pulled the closet door close just in case someone walked in. (My father hired one of his many women as her maid for a birthday gift, but I knew he hired the woman to spy on her).

I walked over to Jameria, taking the bag out of her hands. "I was going to tell you, but I was afraid you would leave."

She looked at me like I said the dumbest thing she ever heard and snatched the bag out of my hand. I snatched it back, throwing it in the corner.

"Look Jameria, I chose you because I knew you would be strong enough to survive. The only other person that ever lived through such tryst was my mother, and as you know, she died during the second birthing," I said, looking directly in her honey brown eyes.

"You don't know if I will survive. Hell, I haven't even agreed to marry you yet."

Okay, this is definitely not going the way I planned.

"Jameria, do you trust me?"

"I did!"

"What do you mean 'you did'? I haven't lied to you about anything."

"No, you didn't lie to me but you didn't tell me *all* of the truth, now did you?"

She started to walk around me and I grabbed her arm. "I *can* promise you that if you choose to marry me, you *will* live through the 'Birthing Ritual.'"

"How?" she said, hesitating a little.

Thank you, God!

"I know you've heard of Kama Sutra."

"Yeah. And?"

"Well it teaches different sexual positions you could use to please your mate or when it comes to the 'Birthing Ritual,' make the mother be as comfortable as possible.

"How's that going to help in the 'Birthing Ritual?'"

I pulled her closer to me to demonstrate as I explain. "Kama Sutra is an art to be mastered." My dick was already hard (it took a *lot* of concentration to make it go down when I'm near her) and started gyrating against her pelvis bone. She let out a little moan.

"There are three main rules in mastering this art," I said, sliding my hands down her firm round ass. I grabbed two hands full and pulled her up so she could wrap her legs around my waist for better access. My dick snuggled comfortably between her thighs, grinding the hot moist flesh it was dying to invade.

I leaned down and whispered in her ear. "The rules are; please your mate, yourself, and to become one with each other," I said, sliding my tongue up her hot throat to her mouth.

To my surprise, she accepted me.

Her full lips were soft, her tongue tasted like strawberries. I pinned her against the wall deepening the kiss and gyrated harder. I could feel her pussy muscles jumping against me.

I was losing control.

I slid my hand between our bodies and touch her there. She moaned again, but louder. I let her down and used my other hand to tease her hard nipples. She untied the strings from around her neck, letting the tiny triangles fall. I took the whole breast in my mouth, suckling like a new born baby.

"Jameria, are you in here?"

The voice was coming from her sitting room. I quickly helped her tie her bikini back in place and straighten our clothes. Just then, Noonie opened the closet door.

"What's going on in here?" she asked, looking from me to Jameria.

69

"Not that it's any of your business Noonie, but I was talking to my mate. It would be considered polite if you would knock next time."

She was about to say something but thought better of it and left.

I turned back to Jameria. "Are you alright?"

She had a glazed look in her eyes.

"Yes."

"Are you still planning on leaving?"

She hesitated before she answered.

"No."

I walked up to her taking both of her hands into mine.

"I promise you—"

I saw something else in her eyes that made me stop. I think it was fear, but I couldn't be sure. That was the one expression I haven't seen her use yet.

"What is it?"

"Nothing," she said dropping her head.

"There is something. Tell me," I said, placing a finger under her chin to see those beautiful honey brown eyes of hers.

"I'm no expert on anything but, I think you are much *bigger* than an average sixteen year old boy."

"Huh?"

She glanced down at my groin area.

"Oh. Really?" I never thought about that.

Suddenly, she froze. "I think I know how all of The Pack's mothers died."

Understanding sunk in. It never occurred to me that the size actually counts.

Ironic.

I need to talk to Uncle Demarcus.

"There's something I need to do. I'll explain later," I said kissing her forehead. Funny how easily that came to me, especially since that was our first kiss.

I went directly to my uncle's wing of the palace. I needed answers. His maid answered the door, after the first knock.

"I need to see Uncle Demarcus."

She led me down the long corridor, into a spacious room with nothing in it but a pool table. He was about to make a shot, until he saw me.

"Tatum. What can I do for you?" he asked with a smile.

"I need to talk to you about something." He must have seen the panic on my face.

"Come into my office," he said, leading the way.

Plaques and pictures covered every inch of the wall behind a large cherry oak desk.

I immediately took a seat in one of the leather chairs, while he made the journey around the oversized desk.

"I think something is wrong." I didn't know how to ask what was really bothering me.

"I don't understand," he said, confused.

I told him about my conversation with Jameria (leaving out the kiss).

He dropped his head. "I should have known your father wouldn't tell you."

Uncle Demarcus never liked my father, because of the way he treated his niece Ky and two nephews.

But my uncle adored us.

He was proud of the way I took responsibility for my little brother and glorified in my intellect.

"You're right. You don't have an average size penis for a boy your age. And if it's already inches from your knee, then you might have the biggest, ever recorded in our history."

Impossible! "But...no one can be *that* big...can they?"

He stared at me for a moment. "Tatum, you're already longer than your father. When he was measured at the last 'Birthing Ritual', his was the largest out of all the Chiefs we've had in our past history."

Then Jameria was right.

"Uncle Demarcus, I'll kill her," I yelled.

"Calm down, Tatum. Look you're a smart kid, who will figure this thing out. Now that I think about it, Jameria's body has changed also. It's like she's become a woman overnight, too."

"What do you mean, 'too'?"

"Come now Tatum. Have you looked at yourself in the mirror lately," he said gesturing at me with his hands.

I knew my body had changed from all of the training, my face lost the baby fat and my skin had taken on a rich cinnamon complexion from being out in the sun so much, but other than that...

"Wait. Is the whole Pack like this?"

"They might be quite the size, but probably not as big as you are."

This might be a first, but I really hate having a big dick. No wonder Jameria looked the way she did. But,

72

before her educated mind kicked in, there was something there between me and my best friend.

"I don't think this will be a problem for you," Uncle Demarcus said, tearing me away from my random thoughts.

"Yeah," I said, standing to leave.

"Tatum?"

"Yes?"

"Your pack might want to find their own mates also. Did you ask them?"

I hadn't thought about that. "No, why do you ask?"

"Because Karden is already sixteen and his father is thinking of having his marriage arranged."

My eyes must have looked as if they were about to pop out of my head. "I'll call a meeting right away. Can you do me a favor, and keep my father out of the View House for a while?"

"Sure, we need to talk to him about some serious matters anyway, starting with, why he didn't tell you about this?" he said in anger.

Chapter Nine

I hurried across the yard, barking The Pack call all the way to Jameria's suite. I didn't knock, just let myself in. Her bedroom door was locked, so I took the key from around my neck and let myself in there too. She was in the shower, so I started pacing across her floor, impatient for her to come out. As soon as I heard the water stop, I went in, and *my damn!*

Jameria was naked.

Her honey bronze skin shimmered in the florescent lighting. Water trickled down between her full breasts, causing my eyes to follow. When they locked on to her hidden valley, my dick saluted her in praise. She was hairless. Though her stomach was flat, her pussy was fat.

I remember a while back—I think I was eleven at the time, when Tyvine stole his father's nudie magazine and it had women in different positions, with their legs spread wide. Back then I thought, 'nice.' But none of them compare to what's in front of me now.

Her Brazilian cut, literally had me foaming at the mouth. I wanted to eat her ass out.

Damn. I really don't need to be thinking about this right now!

"Jameria, put some clothes on. We're having an emergency meeting." She was drying her hair with a big towel but didn't bother to cover up.

Which wasn't surprising.

Jameria and I have been showering together since the very first day she moved here. Though she's my mate, she was my friend first. But now I see what every male eye on the Island sees, and wonder how in the hell I managed to get through so many years without hitting that.

I walked back into her bedroom before I ended up killing her ass.

She came out of the bathroom and went straight to the closet.

"What is the meeting about?" she asked in her Latin tongue.

"Mara is planning to marry Karden off."

"What? What did Karden say?"

"I don't know if he knows yet," I said, walking into the closet after giving her some time to dress. I saw what she was putting on, and went to take a quick shower in her bathroom.

I returned dressed in nothing but white silk loose fitting pants to match her white and gold trim bikini top, with white silk pants. Slits all the way up her thighs.

I always keep clothes of my own here for convenience. It's necessary because the Chief and mate had to coordinate their attire every day. The Pack only had to do it on special occasions.

I went to her vanity table so she could brush out my hair. This was routine. Every day since she told me that

75

she loves running her fingers through my long hair, I made it one of her duties.

"Did you talk to your uncle about anything else?"

I knew what she meant.

"Yes. We'll talk about it later." I stood from her table and went into the bedroom, lifting Coral up and around my shoulders.

Mating season was a month away, so we'll have to let him go soon. Everyone in the palace had gotten used to their Mistress' strange gift and treated Coral like family. Many people were hurt to hear Coral will be leaving us soon.

I took Jameria's hand in mine and went to meet with my brothers. As we entered the courtyard, I could see the Council filing into the meeting hall. My father was one of the last to go in.

He spotted me and started to cross the yard.

"Tatum, hold up. I would like to speak to you for a second."

I slowed my steps to a halt in front of him. "What is it?"

"I wanted to know what your plans were for tonight." He was talking to me, but his eyes were scanning Jameria from head to toe.

Oh, this bastard done lost his fucking mind.

I pulled her slightly behind me and I felt her hand tighten around mine. Coral's head rose from my shoulder, in a striking position facing Motif. He took an automatic step back, and she relaxed a little against me.

"I'm busy tonight. I have to study for exams."

"It won't take long. There is something I have to tell you. Something I should have told you a long time ago."

"Chief Motif, the meeting is about to start," his guard yelled, across the grounds.

"Look, be at my chambers at nine tonight."

"Why so late?"

"I have a meeting to attend later, also." He started back across the grounds. "Don't forget. Nine."

"What was that about?" she asked.

We started to walk again. "Who can explain the dynamics of that man's brain?" I said and she laughed.

When we made it, the entire pack was already there and waiting.

"What's going on, Tatum?" I don't use The Pack call often, so Cole knew something was up.

I looked at Karden.

"What?" he asked.

"Your father is planning your marriage."

"What? Are you sure?"

I nodded. Karden looked as if he would die.

"Don't worry, Karden. He can't marry you off, if we bring your mate here," Jameria said, as if nothing *was* wrong.

"I'm not following you, Mistress."

Jameria took a seat in a blue velvet high back chair. Boaz came and removed the snake from my shoulders and I took the matching seat beside her.

"A while back, I went on the internet trying to find out more about what I can do with the snakes. There was this site about kids with these special gifts of controlling animals."

"That's nice and all, Mistress, but the elders are not going to let us fly all over the world for a girl."

Her smile widens. "That's the best part. One of the kids was a girl who could control birds. I remember it well because she is the same age we are. She lives here. Well not here but on the mainland."

Karden eyes brighten, but his smile faded. "What about her parents?"

"Like I said, it was a while back, but the last I read she was just transferred from another orphanage. Let me do some more research and I'll get back to you tomorrow."

He was still skeptical. "What if my father doesn't agree?"

"He'll have no choice if we can get the girl here before he can plan the marriage," I said.

"I think you're going to have to find me a mate too, Mistress." This was Tyvine speaking.

"I turn sixteen next month."

"Damn. Should I find mates for all of you?" she asked sarcastically.

They all nodded.

"Looks like you're going to have your hands full for a while, but focus on Karden first. The sooner we get her here, the better."

"Fine," she said standing. "I need to go to the library." She spoke to me in her Latin tongue. "Come to my suite later so we can talk." I nodded and she left.

"Why is Council meeting?" Boaz asked.

During my entire dilemma today, I didn't think about Boaz going through what I was going through.

"Boaz, I want you to stay with Cole tonight."

"Why?"

"I have a meeting with father late tonight and there's something Uncle Demarcus wants to talk to you about. Now if there isn't anything else, we can dismiss."

I pulled Karden to the side so I could tell him what Uncle Demarcus told me.

"Why didn't your father tell you?"

"I don't know. That's probably what he wants to talk to me about."

9:28 p.m.

I was sitting in my father's chambers waiting for him to arrive. I'd spent the earlier part of the evening studying Kama Sutra books and that shit didn't do nothing but keep my dick hard. I saw that Jameria was still in the library, so I told her I'll meet her at 9:30. I knew she would be there for a while, since the library doesn't close until ten.

The thirty minutes I was going to give my father, were wasted. I left him a note saying I stopped by.

I decided to go to Jameria's suite, hoping she decided to come in early.

I open the door, flipped the lights on, and there on his knees, peeping through the bedroom keyhole was my father's trifling ass!

"What the fuck are you doing?"

He stood and started fumbling for something to say. "Uh…well…she, she invited me."

"What the hell are you doing in here?" Jameria said from behind me. She had an arm load of books.

Now I get it. Nine o' clock is the time Jameria would normally take a shower and come out naked to her closet.

"You son-of-a-bitch!"

I started toward him, but Jameria beat me there. She spit in his face and kneed him dead in the balls.

Fuck that.

I commenced to whippin' his ass.

Jameria let it go on for a while, before she decided to pull me off of him.

"That's enough Tatum, you'll kill him," she whispered in my ear, as she pulled on the arm that was pounding this sorry excuse for a father into oblivion. She tugged hard and I stood stumbling.

"You are no longer my father," I said, trying to calm my breathing. "You're just Motif to me now. I'm having locks put on all of her doors and if I catch you within ten feet of her, I'm going to kick your ass again."

He can't go to Council because he know he was wrong, so I didn't give a fuck how he was going to get home with two black eyes and probably a cracked skull.

Jameria used her key to unlock the bedroom door, while I kicked Motif's ass out the front. I went into the bedroom, straight to the closet, pulling out a pair of black silk pajama pants and headed for the shower. Jameria had the bedroom door open with a bucket of soapy water and a sponge, cleaning the stains off of the door and hardwood floor.

I stepped under the hot water, thinking what a long fucking day. Just two years ago,

Jameria had just started her period and we both were thinking then 'gross.' Now things *really* don't seem so innocent anymore. I have to admit, I didn't kick my father's ass because he was wrong. I kicked his ass because it was *her* he was trying to look at.

We hadn't talked about it yet, but that kiss is definitely the last conversation I will have today. People have been talking to me all damn day and I haven't accomplished shit.

Jameria came into the bathroom and dumped the water in the toilet. I heard her moving around, then she slid the shower door back and stepped in. This too is normal routine for us because we washed each other's back before the one who stepped in first, leaves.

She grabbed her loafer sponge and soaped it up with her favorite brown sugar body wash and turned her back to mine. I soaped my sponge up again and turned around to wash her back, while she soaped her front. I kept my eyes on the top of her head being careful not to look down. When I was done, I turned back around and she reciprocated, but differently.

Sensually.

She slid the sponge across my back and down my arms. Her right hand traced a line from around my waist and down the center of my chest.

"You know what?" she whispered in her Latin tongue. "That was nice what you did for me."

Her hand circled around my stiff long dick and I shuddered. "He deserved it," I said, speaking in the same tongue.

Her hand started to move back and forward. Damn, that shit feels good!

"What are you doing Jameria?"

"Experimenting."

She pressed her hard nipples against my back and started to jack me off faster. Her lips were soft as they suckled my neck. I moaned, threw my head back, and started to gyrate in her hand faster. I pulled her hand from my dick and pent her ass against the wall. My dick was rock hard and I wanted to fuck her so bad, it actually ached.

I sat her on her feet and shut off the water. She opened the doors and stepped out. I stepped out behind her and went straight to the bedroom door, checking to see if it was locked.

Something came to mind while I had her up against the wall. A woman had to wait ten days after her period to get pregnant. Jameria's cycle ended two days ago. I went back into the bathroom, took the towel out of her hands and dried myself. I stepped into my pajama pants and went back into the bedroom while she finished dressing.

This is also routine for us.

We've been sleeping together since the first day she moved here, but mostly in my chambers.

Jameria came out of the bathroom wearing a black lace gown that came midway her thighs. She slid between the red silk sheets, while I shuffled through her CD's, deciding to let Anthony Hamilton serenade us to sleep.

I hit the light switch and crawled in beside her.

As usual, she had her back to me. I put my arm around her waist and pulled her against me, with my dick nestled between her ass cheeks. Okay, this may be routine for us, but after today's events, this shit will never feel the same to us again.

Jameria's body molded to mine, perfectly. I had my hand on her left thigh caressing it.

"Can we talk now?" she whispered.

I took a deep breath, preparing myself for the last conversation of the day.

"You were right," I began. I told her everything Uncle Demarcus said to me. She listened tentatively, and didn't interrupt.

When I'd finished, she said, "I knew these feelings weren't normal. I'm too young to be thinking of you this way."

Well, at least we were on the same page.

"Don't worry, Jameria. I won't do anything you don't want me to do. We have two more years before the 'Birthing Ritual' and you might decide not to be with me." Though I don't think I'll be able to let her leave so easily.

Her body stiffened.

"What is it?"

"I don't think I'll be able to control myself around you for another two years."

This time I stiffened. "What are you saying?"

She turned over in the bed facing me. "I want to master Kama Sutra with you," she whispered. "As your mate, I should know *all* of your likes and dislikes."

In one day, I had my first kiss, sucked my first tit, and now I'm about to take her virginity with my own.

Chapter Ten

"Are you sure?" I asked.

"I think the only way for me to make it out of this alive, is to practice. When we turn twenty-one and I decide to mate with you for life, I want to be ready." She took a deep breath. "I must admit, since I moved here, I've been having dreams about you. The way you look when you come in from training, with your long hair blowing in the wind, and sweat trickling off every muscle on your body.

"Today was worse. I couldn't even take a nap because the only thing that was on my mind was that kiss from earlier..." Her voice trailed off.

I was speechless.

Jameria had been having sexual fantasies about me for a while. I must be stuck on stupid, or blind not to notice, but she was right. The only way for her to survive this thing, is to practice. There is no rule in the traditional law that said we couldn't be intimate. But I'm sure if we got caught, there will be hell to pay.

There was no light on in the bedroom. Just Anthony telling the world what a good woman he's got. I slid out of bed and flipped the light switch back on.

"Why did you put the lights back on?" she asked.

I walked slowly to the bed. "Because I don't want our first time to be in the dark."

She smiled shyly as I got back in beside her after taking my pajamas off.

Her eyes widen when my dick stood at attention above my abdomen. She reached out to caress it and I moved away. The last thing I wanted to do was explode before I had the chance to even touch her.

There was something else I had in mind.

I stood at the foot of the bed and pulled the sheet off of her body, slowly. She was about to come to me, but I stopped her.

"Don't move, lay there." My voice was low and deep. Shit. When did *that* change?

"Spread your legs for me," I whispered.

Jameria raised her knees, letting them fall to each side.

Damn, she's beautiful down there.

Hell, she's beautiful everywhere.

Her hairless pussy was fat and inviting. For anyone else, a pussy that big would scare any man with an average size penis away... but I wasn't average and neither was she.

I pounced back on the bed like a lion hunting its prey. I leaned forward to taste her and she moaned so loud, I was sure that if someone was walking by her suite, they would surely know what was going on. But at the moment, I really didn't give a fuck. I was eating her out like an all-you-can-eat buffet. The shit just came naturally. There was no fear about what to do next.

As I dined, I felt her thighs shaking around my head.

"Please," she moaned.

That one word alone, nearly drove me insane. I pulled her pearl between my teeth as I inserted two fingers inside her sugary walls.

She lost it.

She screamed so loud, I had to reach up with my other hand to cover her mouth.

I felt her walls contracting against my fingers, as I moved them in and out of her at a rapid pace. Her body arched off of the bed, so I removed my fingers to hold her down, and replaced them with my tongue. She was trying to say something, but it was too late.

Her sweet strawberry juices shot out of her and into my mouth and most of my face. Instead of feeling disgusted, the shit made my dickhead swell. I moved over her, poised at her entrance. I shoved my tongue so deep in her mouth, it tickled her tonsils. She circled her arms around my neck, and reciprocated with her own tongue. I entered her body a little at a time, until I felt her hem break. Then I pushed deeper until my pelvis touched hers. Both of our bodies were shaking by this time, but I held myself in place while her muscles squeezed around me in quick sessions. I don't know how she was able to do it, because my dick filled her to a tee.

I eased all the way out of her slowly, then all the way back in, just as slowly. Her lips were tracing a pattern from my neck to my collarbone, just as my rhythm intensified. I'm not sure, but I think I was possessed by the pussy. I lifted her legs over my shoulders, grabbed on to her slender waist, and started pounding her pussy into oblivion. I know I wasn't hurting her, because she matched my rhythm. Then I felt it.

I was about to cum.

I pounded harder and faster into her, praying that this painful pleasure would find its release. Jameria was on fire.

Her entire body was covered in sweat like my own.

Her inner muscles clamped harder around my dick like a vise. I pinned her legs behind her neck, fucking her so hard, I could smell the blood. Then the relief I'd been looking for, finally came. I threw my head back and shoved so deep inside her, she screamed. I quickly covered her mouth with my own.

We lay there for a while, trying to control our breathing with me still inside of her.

"Are you alright?" I asked, kissing her forehead.

She nodded. "Yes, just a little pain."

I rose, sliding out of her gently. From my stomach to my thighs, I was covered in blood, sweat, and semen.

I looked at Jameria with her legs still parted. Damn, she's beautiful. Her hair was spread over the pillows and her chest rose and fell, causing her breasts to look bigger than the thirty-six C-cups they were. I went into the bathroom and ran a tub of water, then went back into the room and lifted her from the bed. After lowering her in the tub, I changed the sheets, then went back to join her.

She laid her head on my chest after I was seated comfortably behind her.

"We're going to have to go to the mainland to get birth control before we can do this again."

She sighed deeply, with her eyes closed. "We'll get some tomorrow when we go to pick up Kelanie," she said sleepily.

"Who's Kelanie?"

She turned around and straddled my hips, placing her face in the nook between my shoulder and neck. I wrapped my arms around her waist, pulling her closer.

"Kelanie is the girl's name I was telling you guys about. She's in an old orphanage that's standing on its last leg. She'd been in and out of foster homes and the last one burnt down, but it wasn't her fault. The report said it was faulty wiring."

"Do you think she'll come with us?" I asked, running the loafer sponge up and down her back.

She hesitated before answering. "She'll come...because there is no one else in this world to love her."

If it was anyone who knew how it felt to be ridicule because of their gifts, it's Jameria.

She knew what that poor girl must be going through.

"I'll ask Uncle Demarcus to take us to the mainland tomorrow afternoon, meanwhile get directions to the orphanage. I think it will be best if we just take Karden along. After the incident with Motif, I need the rest of The Pack here, to keep their ears open."

We stayed in the tub for thirty more minutes before going to bed. As she slept on my chest, I couldn't help but think, what a perfect way to end your last conversation of the day.

The next morning, Jameria was still asleep when I left. It will soon be time to feed Coral, so my first hunt was for Boaz.

I spotted him, Tyvine, and Cole, sitting by the fountains in the courtyard, watching some type of commotion going on by the meeting hall.

"Hey guys," I called, making my way over to them. "What's going on?"

"Someone attacked your father last night," said Tyvine. Coral was curled around his arm, napping. "His old pack got together to go after his attacker, but he said he didn't even see the guy."

I should have known his bitch ass would come up with some kind of excuse. "Where's Karden?"

"He just went to your chambers looking for you, to tell you what was going on. Do you want me to go get him?"

"No, I'll do it. Coral needs to be fed. Take him back to Jameria's and handle that," I said walking off. "Oh yeah, she's asleep. I left some mice in the sitting room. Try not to wake her."

I met Karden coming out of my chambers. "Dude, I was just looking for you. Did you hear what happened to your dad?"

I told Karden what went down between me and Motif last night.

"*You* did that to him? Damn man, you fucked his face up. But you were right. He's not going to tell anyone who did *that* shit to him."

"He can tell whoever he wants, as long as he heeds my words."

"Trust me, after that ass whipping, he's taking it to heart. I don't think he'll try to go near her again," he said laughing.

"Well, I'm not taking any chances. I want you to have locks put on Jameria's sitting room doors, before we leave."

"Leave?"

I told him what Jameria found out and our goal for today.

"Do you think Demarcus will help us?"

"He's just taking us. Jameria's handling this."

"But she's only sixteen."

Only in age. Something was definitely not right about us. "Yeah, but have you met a person who said 'no' to her yet?" I said grinning.

"You have a point there. But what if the girl—"

"Kelanie."

"Kelanie, huh?" he said with a smile. "Cute. So what if she doesn't agree to the arrangement?"

"She's supposed to have a gift similar to Jameria's, so there's a possibility." No need giving him false hope. "Look, I'ma head back to Jameria's and call my uncle from there."

"Alright, I'll be there in a sec, after I talk to the locksmith," he said, already walking away.

Boaz, Tyvine, and Cole were still there when I made it back to Jameria's.

"Where are Moham and Pierce?" I asked, removing the bedroom key from around my neck.

"Today's their day to feed the wolves." Boaz was flipping through the channels on the flat screen.

91

"Go get them. We're meeting in a few minutes."

I unlocked the bedroom door and saw that the room was empty, but heard the shower going.

She had laid out her beige and cream sundress with beige sandals with ribbons that tie all the way up her calves. Her traveling outfit, because the only way off of this island is by boat. I pulled out a cream color tunic and beige knit pants with brown leather sandals to match. Got undressed, then headed for the shower.

Jameria had just washed the soap out of her hair when I entered, and just as always, we washed each other's back before the first got out.

"The guys are in the sitting room. I'm leaving Cole in charge while we're gone."

She nodded. "Yeah. I'd gotten dressed to go get Coral to feed him. They were already doing it." She turned and looked up into my eyes. "They told me what went on this morning. Do you think he'll send someone for you?"

I smiled. "No. If he does, then I'll have to tell them why I did it. But what if he did? What would you have done?" I said, wrapping my arms around her waist.

She twined her arms around my neck. "You know what I would have done. I'll do it now, if you want me to."

And I believed her.

For the past three years, Motif had kept his distance from me, because Jameria scared the shit out of him. But like my uncle noticed, (not in the perverted way) Motif noticed the changes in Jameria, too. The way her hips swayed when she walked. The way her wavy black hair

92

blew from her slender back, in the wind. How her bronzed skin sparkled in the late Brazilian sun. Something I didn't notice until yesterday. But why am I having these thoughts anyway?

My feelings for Jameria *are* love, but it's different. She *is* me. I *am* her. *We're* one person.

It didn't feel wrong at all, what we did last night. I think it's because of all of the training.

We spend most of the day with each other and stay all night with each other, so that could explain the closeness.

But what about Jameria?

I shoved all twelve and a half inches of myself inside of her, and she took that shit with no fear. I knew the blood came from me breaking her hem, but it still scared the hell out of me. As I look at her now, I knew she had to be mine for life. I don't think there is any woman on this God green earth who can please me the way Jameria did last night, but if there is, I don't want to know her. I'm satisfied with what I've got right here in front of me.

But how does she feel about me?

I had to ask.

"Jameria," I call.

"Yes," she answered. She was drying her hair with a big towel and was about to go in the bedroom. She closed the door back, deciding to lotion her body in here.

"How do you feel about me?" I asked, shutting off the water.

I climbed out and began drying myself off. I couldn't hide my hard dick.

"I love you," she said shrugging her shoulders. "Now put that thing away, we have important things to take care of today."

That's all I wanted to hear. "It's your fault."

I slapped her on her ass, then went into the closet to dress. She followed me in.

"We're letting Coral go tonight," she said quietly.

"What?"

Coral had become so close to me and the rest of The Pack. More than just a pet, more like a dependable friend. But looking at Jameria, I knew she would always be the one who would hurt the most.

I leaned against the table, dressed in nothing but my knit slacks, and dropped my head.

"I understand."

"I know," she whispered with her back to me, tying her sandals.

I knew she knew.

Chapter Eleven

"Is it open?"

We were sitting in front of an old rundown building.

"It's open," Jameria said, climbing out of the car.

She had her long hair in a ponytail and the marks I made last night were visible. But Uncle Demarcus didn't need to see the marks, he already knew.

Karden, Jameria, and I were approaching the yacht, earlier this morning to leave for the mainland. As we were about to board, Uncle Demarcus spotted us and his eyes widened. I had my arm around Jameria's waist, helping her on when he came to me.

We were the same six feet, two inches in height, so when I stood, I was eye to eye with him.

"I need to talk with you," he whispered.

I nodded and left Jameria standing at the railing with Karden.

He started the boat, but didn't move it. I knew what he wanted to talk to me about, so I saved him from asking the embarrassing question and told him that I wasn't breaking any laws.

"Who's to say I can't have a physical relationship with my mate?" I didn't want to come off as whining, but that's *exactly* what it sounded like.

I explained to him that the only way for Jameria to come out of the ritual alive, is that we had to practice. (Over the years, he had made it a point how important her virginity was. But I would have to remind him that even though he's her guardian, she's still mine).

He took a deep breath then let it out. "You'll have to get birth control, so Jameria will have to go to her nurse." I'd hired a nurse for Jameria when I found her maid going through her things.

The first stop on the mainland was the local doctor's office. Jameria allowed her nurse as much freedom as possible. She had a second job on the mainland to volunteer at the doctor's office. After our visit there, the next stop was the orphanage.

Jameria knocked on the old oak door that was splinted and cracked in different places. Minutes later, a Nun answered. From the expression on her face, you'd thought she'd seen a ghost. She stared at the four of us one at a time, with her eyes lingering on Jameria. She crossed herself three times, bowed, and allowed her to enter. My uncle and Karden looked at me, confused. Hell I was confused my-damn-self. I think Jameria was too, but chose not to say anything.

We followed the nun down the dark eerie hall, passing nothing but shadows.

"You've come for Kelanie," she said. My mate and I looked at each other in surprise. "She will not go easily, but someone needs to take her."

She said nothing more, just continued walking until we came upon double hardwood doors, that lead out to a courtyard. The kind you see in prison with high dull gray brick walls on all four sides, nothing but a huge birdbath in the center.

Then we saw her.

She was sitting on the other side of the fountain with her back to us. Her dull black hair touched her shoulders, but her back was stiff as a board. The girl stood and faced us. She had a cinnamon skin tone like ours, with a small waist and thick hips. Her dark brown eyes narrowed when she spotted Jameria.

Jameria's body stiffened next to mine and automatically crouched in front of us, with her arms spread wide. Uncle Demarcus looked to ask, 'What is going on?' but didn't voice it. Karden was about to take her flanks, but she hissed and he took his place back beside me. (My pack took to her hisses, as they did to the Pack Call.)

"You're best to back off, bitch. This is not what you want," Jameria said through clenched teeth.

The girl had circled around and we could see that she was at least five foot six inches. Two inches shorter than Jameria. But unlike my mate, this girl had a flat chest. Not quite a woman yet. Suddenly, a shadow appeared over our heads. It was a big ass vulture with black and red wings descending on us. Jameria moved like lightning, caught the bird of guard and pounced, grabbing the predator around the neck and landed on her feet. She twisted and pulled the head from the now struggling body, and tossed it at the girl's feet.

97

The girl stared in disbelief. I guess she never met anyone like Jameria either. If she knows what's good for her, she's best not to try that shit again. Jameria gave her bird an easy death.

"Now that the games are over, let me introduce myself," my lady said with her beautiful body poised, as if nothing even happened less than two minutes ago. "I'm Jameria Beau, Mistress of Geri Island. This is Tatum, future Chief, his right hand man, Karden, and his uncle and my foster father, Demarcus," she said pointing to each of us. Jameria laid it all out for the girl. She seemed just as intelligent as the rest of us.

Understanding was in her eyes. She looked at Karden with his broad chest and long legs dressed in green knit attire. Then looked down at herself.

Jameria immediately understood.

"Don't worry about anything. We'll go shopping after we take care of things here."

The nun stepped forward. "Don't worry about the paperwork. Just take her," she pleaded.

The girl narrowed her eyes at the woman. "Be patient. I don't want to be here anymore than you want me to." Then to Jameria. "There's nothing here I want. We can leave now."

She didn't look back as the heavy wooden door slammed behind us. Unlike Jameria's departure from her homeland, this girl couldn't care less. The whole time Karden didn't say a word.

When Jameria and Kelanie went in the dress shop, I asked. "What do you think of her?"

We were sitting in a small outside food court, killing time. Uncle Demarcus went back to prepare the boat for departure.

"I don't know. I mean she's cute and all, but…she's nothing like Jameria. She seems wilder, short-tempered."

That was no lie. "You shouldn't compare her to Jameria. That's not fair."

When we met Jameria, she was already carrying herself in a sophisticated way. On her fourteenth birthday, instead of celebrating, she was in the field with the workers, harvesting for a storm that was to hit two days later. An up-standing VIP member of different clubs and organizations that she generously donated to. Something my step-mother claimed is a waste of money.

We went to the jewelry store and purchased a few things for the girls. Karden chose princess cut diamond earrings with a necklace and bracelet to match. I chose a sapphire and diamond tiara with matching necklace, bracelet, and ring.

The two carats of each diamond was beautiful, don't get me wrong. But the detail work of the chain it was suspended from, and the band of the ring, is what made it exquisite. Two thin platinum snakes tangled around each other, encasing each diamond between head and tail.

As we walked out into the street, we saw Jameria approaching with a sexy cinnamon colored woman.

It was Kelanie.

Her once dull black hair now shined with loose curls. A strapless sundress showed off the nice shape of her hips and ass.

"Damn," Karden said walking toward her slowly. From the blush on her face, I could tell she liked her new look.

Karden took her by the hand without saying a word. Kelanie looked at Jameria, but she just walked away to my side. I took her by the hand and kissed it.

She looked back to Kelanie. "He's your mate now. I have no say so. It's whatever he decides and if he decides to keep you or you him, we *will* find a way through this 'Birthing Ritual' mess."

She nodded her head, then turned to Karden. He was still holding her hand.

"Hello, my name is Kelanie Waters. My Indian lineage is Qwataya, of the southern region. I was born April 13th 1988. My mother died giving birth to me, my father gave me up the day I was born, and I don't know if I have any more family still living." Her eyes narrowed. "The nuns said my family hid itself underground from me, because I was evil flying high in the sky."

Karden's jaw clenched. "I'll have them exiled."

And if I hadn't seen it with my own eyes, I'd call myself a liar, but she had that same look in her eyes that Jameria had last night after I kicked Motif's ass.

Desire.

"Uhhh... No. That's alright. It's the past now and anyway, from all I'll have to do, I want to have time to think about it. Jameria told me she's going to teach me as much as she could while you're on your hunt." She said as we walked toward the harbor.

Jameria and I walked a few inches ahead. I noticed how she spoke of my mate with much admiration. But after watching someone kill a three foot tall beast with wings, who wouldn't bow down?

Uncle Demarcus wasn't on the boat when we made it. He left a note saying he'd be back in thirty minutes, 'went to the doctor's office'.

The nurse must have her prescription ready.

Since Uncle Demarcus was Jameria's guardian, he had to sign for them. I sure hope so. What we did last night had been on my mind all day. And she wasn't making it any better in that damn dress. I was hard within seconds.

Not good.

I decided to go to a bookstore I'd seen at the edge of the harbor. Jameria came with me, leaving Karden showing Kelanie around the yacht.

There was an old woman with moles all over her wrinkled face. Her thin gray hair was in a tight bun and she wore an old black faded dress. She was ringing up customers, but kept glancing at us. I'd found the Kama Sutra book I was looking for and Jameria picked up a couple of self-help books for Kelanie.

When we made it to the counter, the woman was looking between us like we were one person. In fact, that's what she said.

"Psymepa. You are one person."

"Excuse me," Jameria said, obviously confused.

The old lady bent down behind the counter and pulled out a black leather bound book that must have seen better days. She opened the book to a painting of a

101

young native man with a spear in his left hand, and a wolf standing on his right side with a green snake on its back.

"Psymepa was the spiritual leader of the animals, but his story is the most tragic. His only job was to protect the animals during mating seasons. To make sure extinction wouldn't happen during his reign.

"Every spring he would appear to see what animals would procreate. One futile spring, he appeared and walked among the forest observing the mates. He came upon a gray and white wolf with a snake on its back," she said looking down at the picture.

"He attempted to remove the thing, but the wolf bared its teeth at him. Then it let out a bark of command and several more wolves and other animals appeared taking each other's flanks. Psymepa couldn't believe what he was seeing. The animals had turned against him because of something that wasn't meant to be. He felt hurt and betrayed. So he left the forest, vowing revenge. He went to the insect people, begging for their help to stop the abomination. The insect people accepted his plea and gave him full control over the arachnid warriors. Eight legged creatures with poisonous webs and venom.

"Not many animals survived after that battle. And though he wanted revenge, Psymepa couldn't bare putting them into distinction. He decided to send some of the animals to different parts of the world. The insect people were upset with him because of his weakness. They tortured him with mosquito and spider bites, and bee stings for twenty days. With his last breath he cursed the insect people, telling them his return will be of the mighty wolf and the vicious snake. No man would stand in his way."

We stood there staring at the breathless old woman. I finally came to my senses and went around the counter to help her to a seat at a nearby reading table.

Jameria stepped up behind my right side. "How do you know about the snakes?"

My pack and I knew she was having a hard time looking for information about her gift.

"And the wolves," the old woman said looking at me. "After you've consummated, it was easier to see. You're just in the wrong bodies."

"Huh?"

"When Psymepa made the curse, he was delirious from all the bites. He said 'no *man* will stand in his way.'"

This lady *cannot* be serious. Could she? I looked to my mate to see what she thought.

Her face was blank.

I saw Uncle Demarcus pass the store window and made our escape.

"Umm...That was an interesting story, Miss, but we must get going." I took out a hundred dollar bill and laid it on the table in front of her. "You don't have to get up for the change," I said, pulling Jameria by the arm.

She stepped forward and placed two more bills in front of the woman.

"I want that book," she said in a stern voice, letting the woman know that no isn't an option.

The molded face woman stared her down and said, "To you, it's free."

Chapter Twelve

The sun had set by the time we made it back to the island. During the ride I approached

Jameria, speaking in our ancient tongue.

"Do you believe what that woman was saying?"

She leaned against the railings, letting her hair flow in the breeze. "I don't know. It *does* seem farfetched, but you must admit that there is something strange about us."

I knew that face all too well. It was her thinking face. Her light brown eyes held curiosity. I cupped her face between my hands and kissed her softly on the lips. I heard Kelanie ask Karden what language we were speaking. He explained to her that it was a language only the Chief and Mistress used to communicate with each other and that she shouldn't ask questions about them... "At least not in public," he said in a low voice.

When the island was in view sight, Jameria removed her ivory cloak and approached Kelanie.

"You will be in hiding until The Pack returns from their first hunt. Karden will take you directly to my suite. I have a sofa bed that's quite comfortable," she said smiling. "After Karden presents you to the Council, you will be given your own suite of rooms. But until then, you will stay with me and I will teach you as much as I can and prepare you for the meeting."

Actually Karden was supposed to train his own mate, but the girl seemed to need a little more taming before Jameria passed her completely over to him.

While Karden escorted her to the suite, Uncle Demarcus pulled Jameria and me aside.

"These will last until the Pack leave for the first hunt. If you have any side effects, let your nurse know immediately. She'll be up Friday."

"Really? I thought I gave her the weekend off," Jameria said, confused.

The blush in my uncle's face told it all. "Actually, I asked her to join me for dinner."

At thirty-eight years old, my uncle literally lives like an old man. He never touched another woman since his wife died in birthing, thirteen years ago. This will be good for him.

Jameria's nurse, Rubea Whitchi, a native woman in her late thirties, traveled during her youth. Her parents were wealthy diplomats of our land, who didn't mind sending their only child all over the world to learn how it worked. She finally had gotten her fulfillment before she decided to come home with her many degrees. I met her at a luncheon at her father's house and hired her on the spot, figuring Jameria would love her. Which she did.

Jameria smiled at him, wished him a good night. I took her hand and lead her to her suite, barking the 'Pack Call.'

Moham and Cole were already there with the new set of keys to the sitting room. I told them to give each member of the pack a key. I was the only one with a key to the bedroom.

Karden introduced Kelanie to the two, then I asked, "Where are Pierce, Tyvine, and Boaz?"

Before Moham could get the first word out, they came walking in one after the other.

Pierce had Coral wrapped around his arm.

"My dad wanted to say goodbye to him," he said sadly.

Jameria dropped her head so I hurriedly changed the subject. "Karden, don't you want to introduce the rest of the Pack?" I turned my back to them, stood directly in front of her and cupped her soft delicate face between my hands and spoke to her in our ancient tongue. "Are you alright?" I asked.

"I don't want to see him go either." She was almost at the brink of tears. Something she hadn't done since she left her homeland.

With her face still cupped in my hands, I called to Karden.

"Let everyone know what's going to happen in the next couple of days with your mate." I notice how Kelanie's eyebrows arched up at the word 'mate.' She'll get used to it. "Bring Coral into the bedroom once you're done."

I took Jameria by the hand and unlocked the bedroom door. She went in, untied her shoes and stretched across the bed. I pulled my shirt over my head, threw it across a chair and crawled in behind her. She maneuvered her body until she was facing me, and then buried her face in my chest. Her tears were hot and her control was slipping. Jameria never showed emotion in front of the Pack or anyone.

"Do you want me to do it with you?" I asked, kissing her hair.

"Yes. I would wait one more day, but it would just lead to another...I cannot deny him this."

Knock. Knock. Knock.

I removed the rubber band from my hair and let it fall over her face.

"Come in."

I told Karden to put him on the bed. Coral glided up and around Jameria's waist and cuddled between us. This time, it was me who couldn't control their emotions. That was his way of saying he will miss us. He only did that move one other time, when Jameria and I went to Tibet to train for ten months with the monks.

"I'm going to miss you too, buddy," I said, pressing his head lightly between Jameria's and my cheek.

This hurt too much. I don't know why, but at that exact moment, it felt like her pain *was* my pain. Not a feeling. More of an artery link.

I rose from the bed and rushed to the bathroom. My chest felt like it was about to cave in. The pain of letting Coral go was so intense, that I had to sit down for a while to catch my breath. Like Jameria, it is going to be hard walking away from him tonight, but it would be wrong not to.

I rose, washed my face, and then went back into the bedroom for my shirt. Jameria was lying in the fetal position with Coral wrapped around her arm face to face.

I kissed her tear-drenched cheek, then Coral's head.

"I'll be waiting in the sitting room when you're ready."

Karden and Kelanie were sitting on the extremely large custom made chocolate suede sofa bed that was on a rise to the left of the room. A small library off to the right and a mini grand piano to the left furnished with two end tables and coffee table that are made of pine wood. The room could be closed off by two double glass doors. The rest of the Pack was seated in front of the flat screen straight ahead.

Boaz saw me approaching the high back chair across from his.

"Noonie wants to have a word with you and Jameria," he said with a grin.

"Say what?"

"Yeah. Cole and Tyvine went to have keys made when she walked through the door looking surprised. I guess she figured no one was here. Anyway she tried to play it off by saying she wanted to speak with you."

She must have new complaints about how people are treating her. I'll never forget the time Uncle Demarcus, caught her with one of the guards. Then had the audacity to offer up her ass just so he wouldn't tell anyone.

"We'll stop by her chambers tomorrow. Was there anymore talk of Motif's attacker?"

Moham shook his head. "No, but the rumors are Motif was trying to talk Mara into marrying Karden off to the Keekulo's daughter." He cast his eyes down at the black marble coffee table. "I hope our Mistress will be able to find a mate for me before I'm next." Then a big grin spread across his face. "I wonder if my mate will be gifted as well…"

"I don't know. Jameria has a lot to do. Train Kelanie, study for her exams, continue combat training and…" I didn't want to tell them about what happened in the book store.

Jameria walked out of her bedroom with Coral wrapped around her arm. Her face was washed clean of the tear streaks, but now it was just a blank.

"Boaz, I want you to stay at Pierce's tonight. Cole. You, Moham, and Tyvine come back in three hours."

Jameria and I left heading straight for the forest. We walked hand in hand listening to the creatures of the night.

"Moham's been hinting around about his future mate," I said grinning.

"Well, his wait won't be long. By the time you guys return from your first hunt, I plan to have Cole's, Tyvine's, and Moham's mate here."

"So you've found them already? When will we be leaving?"

I could tell she was smiling. "Didn't you hear what I said? By the time you come *back*, they will be here…I hope."

"Do you think there will be a problem?"

"No. What I plan to do is ask Elder Demarcus to take Kelanie and me on an education tour of remote places. I also plan to take Rubea with us to keep him company, if she can get the time off from her other job, that is."

We stopped at a cliff near the waterfalls. The full moon made the water sparkle like falling diamonds.

Jameria grabbed a branch above her head and we both watched as Coral glided off her arm and onto the branch. She let the limb slip from her grasp as she back into my chest. I wrapped my arms around her waist as her body shook with sobs.

"Don't cry. You did the right thing," I said with tears in my eyes also.

She turned around and threw her arms around my neck and buried her face there as well. I held her tightly in my embrace. And just like earlier, I felt that same pain. I needed some kind of release. I didn't even realize my tongue was in her mouth, until I heard her soft moan. She must have been looking for the same relief of having to let go of a true and dear friend.

She began kissing down my neck, then my chest, letting her sweet tongue glide over my nipples, then lower to my navel. I threw my head back when she lowered my pants and took the head of my huge hard dick in her mouth. She moaned as she took a little more in each time, until I could fill her soft lips pressing against my pelvis.

Impossible.

I looked down in time to see her pulling back. Watching all twelve inches of me extract from her wet juicy lips. Then I remembered something.

We were fourteen and she was teaching me about different types of snakes. We were in the View House, when she demonstrated with a banana, how an anaconda would open his esophagus and swallow his victim whole. I remembered watching as Jameria let the whole banana glide down her throat. At the time, I thought it was strange she didn't choke to death.

The second time she returned to my pelvis, I held her head there, looking down at her, feeling the inside of her mouth through my dick. As I pulled back out, I saw my entire length wet with her saliva and nearly went crazy. I stroked my dick in her mouth harder, faster, calling to her to grant me relief. She used her right hand to massage my heavy sack, while bracing herself with her left, holding my thigh. I felt her tonsils gliding across my head. I braced my back against a nearby tree and began fucking her in the mouth with all my might. Her lips were bouncing off of my bone as I thrust harder, letting my seed coat her belly.

As I retracted my penis, I noticed strings of semen and saliva hanging from her chin. I was instantly hard again. I took off my shirt and wiped her face. She stood and started walking toward the palace. I grabbed her waist from behind and had her sandwiched between me and the tree. I raised her dress and ripped her black lace thongs off, shoving my dick inside her to the hilt. She rotated her ass as I fucked her against the tree. I wanted more. So I laid her on the soft grass, face down. Wrapping my hand around her thigh, I began rotating my finger on her clit. Her muscles contracted and her juices started to flow.

Jameria's pussy was amazingly hot and slippery. I pounded into her and felt her muscles clinch.

"I'm cumin'. Cum with me Jameria," I whispered in her ear. My cum flowed in waves deep inside her.

I rose, pulling my pants up, then preceded to help her up. We were both filthy and smelt heavily of sex. I made sure no one was in view as we made our way back to her suite.

Chapter Thirteen

The sitting room was empty, and the glass doors to the den were closed with the curtains pulled. Karden came out as Jameria hurriedly entered her bedroom.

"Damn man, what happened to you?" He said, eyeing my dirty clothes.

"Nothing. We had a hard time letting Coral go."

He looked at me confused as I entered the bedroom.

Jameria was in the closet removing her torn, filthy clothes. She had a few scrapes and bruises on her legs and thighs. After I undressed, I took out a pair of blue silk pajama pants to match her sheer, blue gown and matching silk robe, then followed her to the shower. As the water flowed, so did our tears. I needed her again. Our kisses were just as intense as the love we made. I pressed her against the wall, lifted her, and she wrapped her soft legs around my waist.

"I love you," she whispered in my ear.

"I love you too," I whispered back, grinding deep inside.

After we dressed, we went into the sitting room to watch a movie while we waited for Moham, Tyvine, and Cole to join us. Karden and Kelanie were already seated on the black velvet loveseat. I stretched out on the couch, and Jameria crawled up between my legs and rested her head on my bare chest. Kelanie stared at us with shock and surprise on her face.

Karden smiled. "This is routine for our Chief and his Mistress," he explained to her. "They've been close since the first day he went and got her."

She whispered back, "Are you sure they were only thirteen? I mean their bodies are more mature than most adults."

When she said that, I thought about what the old woman said in the bookstore and eyed the old tattered book Jameria bought, sitting on one of the end tables.

The lock on the door turned dismantling my thoughts. It was the guys.

I took the white afghan from the back of the couch, covering us with it. Karden put in the movie, "Friday," while Moham put a bag of popcorn in the microwave. He came and sat on the floor in front of the couch, after placing a kiss on Jameria's cheek (also normal routine), Cole and Tyvine followed suit.

"You wanted to talk to us," Cole said, retrieving the popcorn from the microwave.

Jameria went on to explain to the guys her plans for while we were away on our hunt. Tyvine was the first to speak after she was done.

"How will you keep them hidden until we get back?"

"I have more than enough room, and I don't have to worry about no one coming in here while you're gone." She looked pointedly at Kelanie. "We have eyes watching from above."

Kelanie nodded and then went to the window.

"Is it alright if I open this?"

Karden stepped up beside her and peered out of the window, making sure the coast was clear before he raised it. She stuck her arm out and, seconds later, brought it back in with a grey and white owl perched on it. She whispered something to it, and then held her arm back out of the window where he flew away.

Moham, Tyvine, and Cole had their mouths hanging open.

"Will my mate be gifted?" Moham demanded. He knew he fucked up by questioning his Mistress, but who could deny him an answer with that much excitement in his eyes.

Jameria smiled. "Actually all of your soon to be mates are gifted, that's *if* they agree to come," she said, eyeing Tyvine. His future mate must be a handful. "Anyway, we're leaving the same day you guys are, but returning two weeks before you're due back."

The guys left later that night, excited about the upcoming hunt. Kelanie who'd seen her share of surprises in one day, was once again shocked when I entered Jameria's bedroom for the night. Jameria came in minutes later, cutting the lights off on her way to bed.

"I think we're scaring Kelanie," she said grinning.

I pulled her close, letting my dick nestle between her ass cheeks. "She'll get used to it."

"Do you think the old woman was right? Do you think our souls are in the wrong bodies?" She asked, snuggling closer.

"I don't know. All I know is that I love you more than my own life…and I'll kill anyone who tries to hurt you," I said kissing her cheek.

"That's how I feel about you," she said before she drifted off to sleep.

The next morning, we dressed and informed Kelanie that we would be having breakfast with my father and his wife. "Karden will be here with your breakfast shortly."

Noonie was seated on her red velvet chaise, talking on the phone and quickly made her excuses when she saw us.

"I have to go. My son and his mate just made it."

As soon as she hung up, I lit into her ass. "Noonie, didn't I tell you to stop telling people that you're my mother?"

She acted like I hurt her feelings. Fuck that. This bitch was fucking my father while my mother was still alive and well.

"Tatum, why are you so mean to me? After all I did for you and Boaz, I'd thought you could love me a little," she said, gazing from my feet to my bare chest, lingering longer below the waist.

Jameria saw what her eyes were focused on and stood directly in front of me. I wrapped my arm around Jameria's waist and pulled her gently against me.

"You left word that you wanted to speak with us," she said in her authoritative tone. When it came to Jameria, Noonie had to choose her words carefully and always spoke to her with her eyes cast down.

"Yes...I would like to invite the Keekulos' to the palace for a welcome home party we're giving the Pack after they return from their first hunt," she said looking up with a smile.

I was about to protest, but Jameria said 'fine', then turned and walked out.

"What was that all about?" I asked her when we made it outside. "You know why she wants the Keekulos' there."

"Yes I do. But by the time you return, I'll have my own set of guests there as well," she said grinning.

~~~

Two weeks later, we were all prepared to go. Jameria, Uncle Demarcus, Kelanie, and Rubea' would leave later tonight, to keep their identities concealed. Karden stood by the sitting room door saying his goodbyes to Kelanie. He leaned in and kissed her lightly on the lips. She blushed, stepping back to let Jameria and I exit.

The people of Geri came out to wish us well on our first hunt.

I kissed Jameria at the edge of the woods, not caring who was looking. Her tongue tasted so sweet that I didn't want to let go.

"I love you," I whispered with my forehead pressed against hers.

"I love you too. Be careful," she said with tears in her eyes.

I quickly wiped them away so none of the people would see her showing emotions. I stared down into her face, watching it go blank.

"You be careful as well." I noticed how some of them were watching with questions in their eyes.

Thank God for rules.

I don't think Jameria nor could I explain what was really going on between us. I turned and entered the woods with my pack for our first hunt. We would be gone for two months searching for the most deadly prey known to man. Bring it back to the palace, proving that we are men. But as we made our way deeper into the forest, I felt Jameria's expedition will be more demanding than ours.

Chapter Fourteen

We've been gone for one month and three weeks when we finally caught our third hyena. We were tired, dirty, smelly, and *I* was horny as hell.

I needed my mate.

Not a night went by, when looking up at the stars thinking about the love Jameria and I made together. The night before we parted, she rode my dick like a bucking horse and I welcomed it.

Karden looked like I felt.

He'd told me, him and Kelanie kissed and made out a lot, but hadn't gone further than that. But from the look in his eyes, I think they're going to be doing a whole lot more than kissing and touching.

Moham was more anxious to get home than the rest of us. In fact, our first week in the woods, he was ready to go home.

"I think we should go back and help the Mistress track our mates."

I told him we have our jobs to do and Jameria has hers. "She doesn't need our help anyway.

"Kelanie is helping them along the way."

We trotted through the woods with our kill on three long branches.

"I think we're lost," Karden said randomly. Just then, a blue humming bird flew pass me and landed on his shoulder. "What the hell-." The bird flew forward before he could finish his sentence.

"I think we should follow it," Boaz said taking the lead.

We followed the bird for a couple of miles until we saw Jameria's two big ass anacondas raised their heads in welcoming, eyeing our kill. I let my hand glide along the black scales of its back.

"You can have it after we've shown it to Council."

We burst through the opening of the woods relieved to be on familiar grounds. The humming bird flew directly to Jameria's den room window and pecked on it. The curtains moved slightly, but that was short lived, because we were ambushed by a crowd of people.

"They're back," someone yelled.

Within one minute we were surrounded. I felt someone grab me around the waist. I immediately thought it was Jameria but was disappointed when I saw Noonie.

I pushed her away from me. "Oh Tatum, I'm so happy you guys returned today. I just had the Keekulos' shown to the guest quarters. We will have the party today."

"Whatever," I looked around searching for my mate. Damn, I miss her. Where is she?

"Tatum," Uncle Demarcus called. He'd just hugged his son and was approaching me. "I knew you boys could do it. I'm sorry...*men*," he corrected. He hugged me and slipped a piece of paper in my hands.

It was from Jameria.

Hi luv,

I miss you so much, and I can't wait to see you, but there is something I need you and The Pack to do before Noonie starts her party. We'll meet you there after you guys have bathed and dressed. I left outfits for each of you in your chambers. Luv you 'til death.

Jameria

I told Karden what was up so he could spread the word on to the rest of The Pack. Before we could leave, Council came out and surveyed our kill, deeming us approved.

"I'm quite sure you guys are ready to celebrate," Mara said with his arm around Karden's shoulder.

Before I could answer, Motif came to congratulate Boaz and me.

"You boys did well," he said, hugging Boaz. Then he looked at me as if for the first time. "Tatum, I hadn't noticed how big you've gotten. You and your young mate are growing so rapidly."

I narrowed my eyes at him, wondering what he was up to.

"Noonie has put together a wonderful party for you boys. A few young ladies from the Keekulo tribe are here to help you celebrate," he said eyeing a nervous Mara.

"Yes...Er, Karden, I need to have a word with you-"

Karden picking up on the exchange then cut in. "Let's talk later dad. I would really like to take a long hot shower," he said already walking away.

We followed suit, going to our own chambers.

An hour later, I met The Pack in my sitting room, wondering if their attire matched my urban gray silk loose fitting pants with matching open robe, which hung below the back of my knees. Jameria had bought me a set of two carat princess cut diamond earrings in platinum, as a welcome home gift.

Though our styles were the same, the colors weren't, but still matched somehow. Boaz and Pierce wore an aqua color that reminded me of Aruba. Tyvine, Karden, Moham, and Cole all wore blue, but of different shades. One darker than the next.

"I hope Jameria has a plan," Karden said locking the door behind him. "Man, there are a lot of people out there. How will they know which girl to talk to?"

"I'm quite sure she knows what she's doing." Every one of them looked nervous. "Look you don't necessary have to pick the girl Jameria brought for you to meet. The point is to mingle and see what catches your eye."

The beach was crowded. We descended down the hill and everyone cleared. I spotted Jameria in her gray and silver skirt with splits up each thigh. A silver bikini top made her beautiful glitter coated breasts sparkle. Her long thick black shiny hair was parted in the middle, making waves on each side down to the diamond belly chain around her thin waist. Those honey brown eyes of hers finally landed on me and she smiled. God, I missed her.

123

Several people tried to stop me, but I wasn't having it. Neither was she. My tongue was in her mouth before I had time to comprehend that we were surrounded by hundreds of people. She pushed me gently in the chest to break to kiss, then spoke in our ancient tongue.

"Yeah, I missed you too. How was your hunt?"

I spoke back in the same tongue. "Boring. I've been thinking about you the whole time.

"Did you feed the wolves?" I'd taught her how to feed our most sacred animal the first night after Council.

"Yes, and I need to talk to you about that."

People were staring at us, probably wondering what in the hell kind of language that is.

"Let's go to a table. How was your trip? Were you successful?"

I looked around and saw a lot of girls who looked like kids compared to us. Even younger than Pierce and Boaz. Only a few stood out.

"Oh yes," she said grinning. "But the guys have to make their own choice. I want this to be fair. Now about the wolves," she said, still speaking in our tongue. "Remember that book I bought. Well, I read this part about a hibernated state. It's like a gift that's asleep that has to be waken." She saw the confusion on my face. "If what that old woman said is right, that means you share the same gift of animals. The leader of the wolves.

"In that book, it spoke of a mighty wolf pack, which protected the land. The Pack consists of seven male wolves, one standing at center point. The leader. He appointed each wolf a certain animal to watch over. He took the most poisonous and dangerous one and became very close to the worlds enemy. Showing the wolf through the snake eyes how the world would rather kill it than embrace it. Why it strikes first and asks questions last. Psymepa only showed during mating season and the animals needed protecting from savages and hunters who would only kill for a prize.

"Tatum, I think I've found the leader of each animal but one," she said staring at me.

Before I could reply, commotion was coming from the other end of the beach. It was Motif, Noonie, and Mara facing Karden and Kelanie.

"Is there a problem here?" Motif looked at me nervously.

"Well, I was just saying to young Karden that it would have been nice if he had let us know he had a young lady friend."

"She's my mate," Karden said his jaw set firm. "We'll meet in front of Council on Monday." He took Kelanie's hand and walked back to our table with me.

"What was that all about?" Jameria asked.

"The Chief wanted to know why we were dressed alike." Kelanie wore a strapless sheer dress that stopped midway her thighs with the diamond set Karden bought her as a welcoming gift. "I guess that kiss set it off," she said blushing.

Karden smiled, pulling her close around her waist. I noticed how her once flat chest was starting to grow. Karden definitely noticed. Her curly hair was piled on her head in loose tresses, exposing her long neck. Yeah, Karden is satisfied.

125

Cole and Moham showed up with girls who wore shades similar to theirs. The girl Cole was with was pretty with green eyes and long dark hair. Her name was Maria Santos from Mexico; her tribal lineage is of the Curry people. Moham was holding hands with a girl whose complexion was nearly white with very pink lips. But her straight black hair and high cheek bone gave away her heritage. Her name, Tyce Kendrix, from Canada. Her Indian lineage was of the Mighty Bear people. Her body was toned and beginning to take on a woman's shape.

Tyvine arrived last at the table with a wild looking girl whose thick red hair was bundled in long spiraling curls, making her cat eyes glow. Her thigh high dress that matched his, fit snugly to her curvy body. Her name, Cougar, from Madagascar. Her parents lost her in the woods. Jameria later found out her parents died, looking for her. She's of the Macaat tribe.

Noonie came to our table pissed.

"I'm sorry, but I didn't invite you here. Where are you from?"

Jameria trained them well. Each mate looked to their significant other and Noonie's eyes nearly popped out of her head. The guys nodded in response smiling. She walked away before the young ladies started to speak.

Jameria sighed. "I guess this is where the drama starts. Party's over," she said rising. I rose as well, as Motif and Noonie approached.

"I'm sorry, but I'm going to have to ask you to leave," Motif said looking at each girl sternly.

126

"No they don't. I invited them," Jameria said moving in front of the table.

"You had no right. Noonie put this party together. Not you. Now I want them gone immediately," he said raising his voice to my mate.

Had he lost his mind? I had to ask.

"Have you lost your damn mind? Don't raise your voice to her. As a matter of fact, you forgot the rules are ten feet away," I said, making my point clear.

He cleared his throat. "I don't want to fight with you right now Tatum, but your mate has crossed the line."

"And what line is that? There's no law about who you can and can't invite to a party."

"Besides," Moham said standing and smiling. "These are our mates, not dates," he announced.

Noonie nearly fainted.

"What have you done?" Motif approached Jameria with his hand raised high. I moved in front of her and he slapped me instead.

Then all hell broke loose.

Chapter Fifteen

Jameria jumped high in front of me and wrapped her legs around Motif's neck, flipping back on her hands throwing his body into the cakes and pies. Then wheeled back and crouched in front of me. Each girl who was at the table took her flanks. Motif couldn't believe his eyes. He used his old Wolf Call for his retired pack.

I couldn't believe he did that shit.

My pack automatically took their mates flanks. Jameria hissed and Kelanie let out a loud bird call. A deep rumbling sound came from Maria and Cougar let out a growl that would put the purest cat to shame. Tyce hit her fist together. We felt the ground rumbling beneath our feet as bears, cats, apes, birds, and snakes of different kinds surround the Council. No one moved. Jameria's anacondas surrounded us in a cocoon.

"You best to back the fuck off Motif. This isn't what you want."

My big bad ass father, the Chief of the tribe, pissed in his pants. His pack eyed the vulture over our heads and began backing away. The bears and lions began roaming and everyone at the party scattered.

"Tatum," my Uncle Demarcus said smiling. Obviously, happy with the entertainment.

I placed my hand on Jameria's shoulder. She rose and the other girls followed suit. She nodded to Kelanie who whistled twice and the animals dissipated.

Jameria turned to me. "We have to start preparing you," she said in our ancient tongue. "Before I kill your father!"

"Get in line."

People began leaving the party when the animals left. I looked at each of my pack members to see if this shit scared the piss out of them too. They looked more than happy. Moham was practically bouncing.

Uncle Demarcus came to our table as we was about to leave.

"Council would like to meet with you Monday morning," he said to the Pack. He looked to Cole and smiled. "I'm sorry for having the chance to meet your mate before you did, but I was hopeful." Cole smiled back and nodded.

"Come to my suite when you're done here," Jameria said to her now growing female pack.

"Escort them," I said to my own, taking her hand.

Noonie was there waiting with her own complaints. Jameria unlocked the door to the sitting room.

"Where did you find those...girls at?" Noonie said, choosing her words carefully. "Because Tatum was disobedient in choosing you, doesn't mean the whole pack has to follow suit."

"Watch it Noonie," I warned her. "Anyway, they *chose* those girls. I guess you'll just have to deal with it."

"Motif won't let this happen," She said starting to leave. "You're missing out on a good opportunity."

"Which opportunity is that? More land to be in control of, or more places you can go to give your pussy away?"

She walked out slamming the door behind her. Good riddance.

I locked the door and picked Jameria up in my arms, cuddling her close on the couch.

"I missed you," I said, kissing the tip of her nose, then her lips.

She tasted so sweet. My tongue glided across her lower lip. She wrapped her arms around my neck, deepening the kiss. We were still kissing when we heard the locks turn. Jameria was still seated on my lap as the group filed in.

"Okay, I really need to ask a question," Karden said pacing the floor. "What the hell just happened back there? Here's the biggest question, why the *fuck* didn't I freak out...I mean...it felt...comfortable. Shit like that should not feel comfortable!"

"Calm down. There's no need to panic. Jameria will explain everything to you later, but right now we need to prepare for the Council meeting."

Karden wasn't far from the truth. Our bodies actually moved like animals out there, and the feeling was so natural, it came to us without thinking.

Jameria got up and went to Boaz and Pierce taking both of their hand into hers.

"I'm sorry that I won't be able to bring your mates here yet, but they are anxious to meet you." She pulled them forward to her bedroom and we all followed. She opened the top drawer to her cherry oak cider chest and took out two pictures of very beautiful young girls.

"I can't let you keep the pictures because Noonie and Motif are going to be watching you closely," she said, mainly to Boaz. "But they are preparing themselves as your future mates."

"What's her name?" Boaz said, holding the picture of the honey brown skinned girl with thick long black hair that was in a single braid. Her eyes were hazel.

"Shyamae Boyd. Yours," she said pointing to the picture of a girl a shade lighter in Pierce's hand. "Carmen Joyce, her gift is the sea creatures. I promised their parents safety for the girls. Just like us, they are both homeschooled and smart for their age."

"What can Shyamae do?"

Jameria smiled and it lit her honey brown eyes. "She can control the four elements; fire, wind, earth, and water. It would be too dangerous for us if we had them here right now. Motif would say you're too young and have the girls sent back. And their parents have to prepare themselves of never seeing them again."

"So when *will* they be able to come?" he asked, anxious like Moham. Boaz had always taken to the animals, but his first time watching Jameria control snakes, she became like a surrogate mother to him in one day.

"The day before Pierce's thirteenth birthday."

"Why so long?" Pierce whined.

"Because you have to prepare yourselves for them as well." They all looked at her, confused. She went on to

131

explain about the woman in the bookstore and the book she bought.

"So we're sleeping wolves, whose jobs is to protect a certain animal," Tyvine said looking even more confused.

"In a way, but you're not protecting the animal itself, but the carrier," she said looking at each female.

"So Tatum's gift must be more potent than ours because *he* found you," Karden said nodding to himself.

Moham with his mates hand still in his, moved forward. "What do we need to do?"

"Here's the problem. We have enemies, called the Insect People. I imagine, instead of fighting real insects, these will be real people. I looked on the internet and saw that these people control grasshoppers, spiders, mosquitoes, and other poisonous insects, which is also the name of their fighting skills that they've mastered in. Such as the Flying Mantis who is their leader."

"What does that have to do with us?" Karden asked.

"Well, in the book, when Psymepa banished the animals, he took away the leader of the wolves' sound voice and put it in an old dull blade, and gave it to the Insect People for his betrayal.

"For centuries the Insect People have been hosting a National Martial Arts Tournament, 'The Dragon's Death.' And the prize has been the knife. They never lost, so the knife is still in their possession. They have the tournament every three years."

"When is the next tournament?"

"Three years from now," she said looking directly at me. "It's too late for us to enter this year, but that's fine because we have a lot to prepare for if we're planning to get that knife."

Knock. Knock. Knock.

Jameria quickly took the pictures back and stuff them in her top drawer, while we all filled back out into the sitting room. When I answered the door, it was my father and Mara with a nervous look on his face. (That's becoming his normal facial expression now.)

"May we come in?"

Jameria came and stood directly in front of me. "That ten feet goes both ways. Elder Mara can come in, but the next time you step a foot in here, I'ma go Roots on your ass," she said through her teeth. I wrapped an arm around Jameria's waist to let Mara enter.

"I just wanted to have the chance to introduce myself personally to the mates of The Pack," he said smiling at everyone in the room. "I've never seen such a large group of gifted young women. Boaz, Pierce, I hope our young Mistress can find you two mates as gifted as this bunch."

What the fuck is he up to? Fishing. I looked to Karden who had the same look on his face that was in my head. Boaz nor Pierce responded, so he turned his attention to Karden.

"I think a proper introduction is in order," he said bowing to Kelanie. "Hello, I'm Mara Poteece," he said quickly in Portuguese. "Pleased to meet you and I hope you will be ready for Council."

So that's what this was all about. They were testing the girls to see if they spoke our native tongue. I think he's playing dumb today, because I knew he could tell that the girl was a native from the mainland. But it wasn't Kelanie who spoke. It was Tyvine's mate, the wild one named Cougar who responded in three different languages, including our own.

"It's nice to meet you Elder Mara and we are so looking forward to the Council Meeting," she concluded in French. Tyvine, who was sitting in the window seat beside her, wrapped an arm around her neck and pulled her in for a kiss on the forehead.

"If you don't mind Elder, my Pack and I just got back from a long expedition and we haven't seen our mates in a long time. Can we please have some privacy?" I said, opening the door where Motif remained standing.

"Okay Mistress, how are we going to have time to train for a tournament, train our mates for the 'Birthing Ritual,' school work, chores, and preparing for Pierce and Boaz's mates, and keeping all of this from Motif, Noonie, and Mara," Moham said smiling. Obviously happy about the challenges ahead.

Her answering grin was all they needed to see.

Chapter Sixteen

Two years later…

My pack and I watched as the yacht approached, bringing our mates back to us after their two week summer vacation. (At least that was the ruse they left with.) Their first week was spent in America, shopping (picking up Carmen, Pierce's mate.) Then spent their last week in Australia on hiking expeditions (picking up Shyamae, Boaz's mate.)

For the past couple of years, we've been planning and preparing for this very moment.

Each of my pack members learned their mates and gifts well. Including Pierce and Boaz. Jameria and I would take them on trips to visit and learn their mates and meet their parents. They even sent their future mates gifts on special occasions. As far as schooling for us. Jameria and I decided to continue online classes and private tutoring until next year when we will both be attending Harvard. Our main focus was the tournament.

The only female who didn't go on the trip was Cougar, Tyvine's mate. It seems the only person who could control the cat girl was him. She wasn't as rational as the other girls had become. The smallest bit of trouble and mountain lions and Jaguars would come running. Jameria did her best to try to control the girl. She's the strongest out of all of them, but after killing twelve cats, she just gave up. Cougar had to be tamed.

At the age of sixteen, Tyvine and Cougar lost their virginity. And he laid it on her wild ass too. One day he was teaching her how to feed the wolves, and that one hiss at them, nearly drove him over the edge.

"Cougar, if you don't cut that shit out, I'ma put you in the cage with them," he warned.

Karden and I were close by, walking the horses back to the stables.

She looked as if she wanted to laugh. "And what the hell can a *dog* do to me?"

He stared at her for a moment, then snatched her ass toward the wolf pin. Karden was about to protest but I grabbed his arm to keep walking. That shit was between Tyvine and his mate. It was bound to happen.

Instead of Tyvine locking her in, he went in behind her and locked the gate.

"What are you doing?" she asked.

"I'ma show you what a dog can do." He grabbed her hand and walked to the back of the pin pass the wolves, then pushed her over one of the dog houses and raised her animal print mini up around her waist.

"If this is supposed to be my punishment, then what do I get for killing one?" she said sarcastically. Tyvine shoved his dick in her so hard, Karden and I both jumped from the pain she must be feeling.

Hell, we heard it.

She screamed so loud her cats came running. Two panthers and a jaguar. The wolves were on their feet in defensive positions.

Tyvine was still pounding the shit out of her pussy. "Call them off," he yelled at her, then slapped her hard on her ass. She screamed again and the cats bowed down, covering their ears with their paws. He leaned down whispering something before taking her earlobe into his mouth. The cats went back to the woods. By this time Jameria, Cole, and Kelanie joined us to see what the commotion was all about.

"I'll be damned," Jameria said shaking her head. "If that's all it took to tame that girl, I would've had him do that sooner," she said heading back to her suite.

When Tyvine was done, he told her to, "Feed the damn wolves and stop fucking with them." She fell to her knees panting. Understanding was in her eyes, the type of hold Tyvine had on her. "Now you see what a dog can do." We'd found out in our physical that the shortest penis amongst our pack was ten inches, and Boaz and Pierce were fourteen at the time.

We didn't have any more problems out of her ass since then. Whenever she did act up, we called Tyvine on her ass. But unfortunately, it had its down falls. Because Jameria couldn't pack Tyvine's dick in a suitcase to shove in Cougar's mouth to keep her in her place, Cougar had to stay behind because Tyvine had to train with the Pack for the upcoming hunt. He would've let her go with them, but she was just too wild to let loose on society.

But the trip was short and my baby was back and smiling down at me in her white silk skirt with gold trimming down to her ankles. A white bikini top supported her full breasts.

Over the past three years as she trained with her snakes, her body seemed to move as one.

And DAMN! She's sexy. Whenever she walks through the courtyard, every male eye turns to stare. But it doesn't bother me none. They can look but touching would be deadly.

She came down the ramp and into my waiting arms. And my tongue was in her mouth instantly. I stopped caring a long time ago if anyone found out that we were having sex before marriage.

To look at my pack and not tell would be ludicrous.

We did get the usual complaints and then some. But as usual we were all ready to stand before Council once again for our actions. By uncle Demarcus being guardian of all the girls, he granted us permission to date his wards, as long as we were being safe and since it wasn't against traditional rules. Other people felt we were setting a bad example for the children of future pack members. Like I gave a fuck. But Jameria argued that if they don't educate themselves on the matter, there would be no way to survive the ritual. Council granted us permission as well, saying that if one of the mates gives birth before her eighteenth birthday they would be dishonored from the pack. Which they had put into writing.

I walked her back to her suite as planned, taking the attention away from the boat.

"Did you get the girls?" I asked in our ancient tongue.

"Of course. Tatum, I have to tell you something about one of them." She was looking straight ahead but her eyes were guarded. I unlocked the sitting room door where Boaz and Pierce sat patiently waiting. They got up and kissed their Mistress' cheek while I unlocked the bedroom door.

"She was successful," I said before they had a chance to ask. I pulled her in the room, closing and locking the door behind me. I didn't care what she had to say, as long as she was saying it with me inside of her.

I pulled Jameria's fine ass in the bathroom, sat on the toilet and started undressing her.

"The pack is going to have to make at least two trips for Shyamae's things, thanks to Boaz and all that shit he sent her over the years." Then she smiled. "But I'm not mad. She belongs with Boaz."

We all knew that. Every year for her birthday, other kids would bring games, or little knick knacks like that. Boaz always gave her diamonds. There's no tradition behind it, but the pack only give gifts like that after they've been announced to Council. Not Boaz. On her last birthday, he bought her a custom made diamond studded cell phone. They talked every-damn-day. I had to literally put his ass on a schedule.

"We'll handle it later," I said, allowing my eyes to roam around her curvy body. "But right now, we'll take a shower and go have dinner."

"Oh, is that all we're doing?" she said, stepping between my legs and gyrating in front of me in order motion.

I pulled her white silk thongs to the side, licked then kissed her sweet clit. "I thought the rest was obvious," I said standing, removing my pants. She grabbed my shoulders then straddled my waist. I braced her against the wall, angling my dick to enter her tight pussy.

I fucked her up against the wall, asking her, "Whose pussy is this?" while I shoved two of my fingers in and out of her tight ass. Over the years, Jameria and I mastered the art of Kama Sutra, that she welcomes the anal play with a passion. I couldn't believe she loved me shoving all this dick in her tight ass. And I welcomed it as well.

I wasn't ready to cum yet, so I pulled her in the shower with me and turned the water on. I turned her face forward toward the opposite end of the shower. "Relax your muscles baby," I said, pressing her chest to the wall so I could have easy access to her anus.

"Yesssss," she said in response, getting into her favorite position. My dick came to my chest now and ever since the first time I bust her ass open, she kept begging me to dig in there again and again.

I fucked her there while I had all four of my fingers in her pussy pulling her harder on my dick. She spread her ass cheeks when I grabbed her hair and started going at it like a dog in heat. At seventeen her libido was on fire. She got off my dick and took it to the head while she dug her fingers up her pussy. That shit turned me on so much, I grabbed her head between my hands and started fucking her face. She used her right hand to pull me deeper into her mouth. I felt her tongue lift under my balls while my dick was all the way down her throat. Her esophagus was squeezing in sessions around my dick, while maintaining control of her breathing.

She learned well from her snakes.

She fitted both balls in her mouth with my dick and began suckling. I felt that shit all the way to my ass. She took the four fingers she had stuck up in her pussy and stuck them in my mouth so I could suck her juices off. Her middle finger on her right hand was rotating in and out of my ass, with my balls rotating on her tongue, while sucking my dick. I rotated my ass on her finger, grinding my pelvis against her face. Cum shot down her throat in waves. She retracted her finger from my ass and my long dick from her swollen lips. I braced myself against the wall to control my shaking and catch my breath. Jameria sat on the marbled floor of the shower and spread her legs wide, bracing a foot against the shower door and one against the wall. Cum was shooting out of her pussy by inches. Whenever I bust a nut in her mouth, it made her cum, which made my dick rock hard again.

"Fuck the shower," I said, cutting it off and taking her hands, pulling her up. We went into the bedroom and I told her to get under the covers while I knocked on the bedroom door.

Karden came immediately. He knocked back and I cracked the door. "Clear the room for me and lock the door. Tell the pack we'll meet for dinner." I needed the sitting room clear for what I have in mind.

I closed the door and went to the bed removing the covers. I went to her bedside table and handed her the bin-woe balls and ties. She got on her knees and started tying one of her wrist to the bedpost. I tied her other hand for her and gagged her mouth with a silk hanker and tied it in place using one of my silk ties, so no one could hear her scream. This too was one of her favorite positions.

I learned this one night in the Himalayas, when we were stuck in a cave with no heat. Just a log fire, a sleeping bag, and two naked bodies. Surprisingly, we weren't stuck in an avalanche as loud as she was screaming.

I inserted the balls in her pussy while I ate her ass out. She moaned pressing her chest to the mattress, arching her back, raising her ass higher. I didn't waste no time. I shoved my dick in her ass to the hilt. She bucked forward like a wild horse. The bin-woe balls was rubbing her g-spot against my dick. I wrapped a hand around her thigh and used the other one to grab a hand full of her thick hair. I was pounding into her so hard that her ass cheeks were bouncing off my abdomen like a basketball. Her left ass cheek started to shake and I knew she was having another orgasm. She collapsed flat on her stomach, but I was still going at it. I was out of control. My teeth clamped down hard on her shoulder as I tried to push my whole fucking body in her ass.

She gurgled a scream and that shit made my cum flow.

I held myself deep inside her, while I untied all of her bindings. I removed the bin-woe balls last giving her time to clench her muscles to keep her juices from spilling out. Then I removed my dick slowly, pulling her up onto her knees before I climbed off the bed to watch *my* favorite position.

She spread her ass cheeks and pussy lips, and I had the pleasure of watching our juices squirting in puddles from her ass and pussy at the same time.

Damn, that shit was beautiful!

I'd fuck her again if she wasn't already headed for the shower.

Fuck that.

I had her ass on the bathroom counter working my dick in her sweet pussy, like a man possessed. And she didn't mind one bit.

After we took a shower, she took a nap while I went to hunt for Karden. Something about us just wasn't right. What Jameria and I did back there was not just man and woman. That shit was animal instinct. I could *smell* her. Had me to the point that if I was a dog, I'd be clawing at the door to get to her heat. Shit, I wanted to go back now. What the hell is wrong with me?

Karden wasn't in his chambers or the library courts. I would use the pack call, but this is personal. Though I know they are not supposed to question me or my mate, but we're much closer than that now. We trust each other, but Karden has been there from the very beginning and has always been on my level.

I went back to the north wing where the women are housed, to Kelanie's suite. I used my key to her sitting room, then knocked on her bedroom door. All the women bedroom doors is made of heavy oak, so I couldn't tell if he was in bed or in the shower.

He finally came to the door with his long black hair hanging down his bare chest, a blue silk sheet wrapped around his waist. A bite mark was starting to show just below his navel.

"Sorry man, didn't mean to bother you. Come to Jameria's suite when you're done."

"It's cool. I was just about to take a shower anyway. Kelanie's asleep. I'll be down in fifteen minutes."

Fifteen minutes later, Karden entered the sitting room with blue silk loose fitting pants and matching robe on. "What's up man?"

I told him what happened as soon as Jameria got off the boat and how I felt. "I mean, I don't know what happened. When we went on hunting trips months at a time, it was never this intense, except..."

"Except," he said.

Jameria and I never mentioned our time together when Coral had to leave. I mean, people know we have sex, but that day was a happy day for Karden because he got his Kelanie. But for Jameria and me, it was personal. So we kept that between us. As it will remain.

"Nothing." He really didn't expect an answer. His mind was on something else.

"Do you believe that stuff Jameria was saying about that Psymepa guy?" His dark brown eyes bore holes into mine.

I answered him truthfully. "Ever since we met Jameria, we knew she was trying to make sense of what she can do and why. I think if this proves right then a lot

144

will be explained, but if not it will just be back to square one with her."

He looked down for a moment, then back up at me. "I think she's right."

This time I was the one staring.

"You said you smelt her. Tatum man, that shit happened to me too. Man, I thought I was going to lose my mind. If you hadn't knock on the door when you did, I would've hymned Kelanie's ass up again. I'd already woke her up three times." He said this in a sad tone. "But it felt so natural."

That's when something in my head clicked. "Boaz."

Karden looked at me with wide eyes. We ran out of the sitting room closing and locking the door behind us, to Shyamae's suite. I unlocked the door and was relieved to see Boaz sitting at her desk with the traditional rule book. Pierce and Carmen were on the couch with a Portuguese language book on her lap and Shyamae fixing glasses of juice.

"What's wrong?" Pierce said standing. Must be the fucked up expression on my face.

Boaz followed suite.

"Nothing," I said relaxing my posture some, so they wouldn't be alarmed. "Just wanted to tell you we're having dinner here with the girls."

"Oh, Karden already told us," Boaz said looking confused because Karden was standing right next to me.

"Just making sure," I said closing the door. "Shit man. I'm freaking out."

"Yeah. But you have a reason to."

Chapter Seventeen

Jameria was already up when I went to get her for dinner.

"Noonie stopped by with an announcement. We've been invited to Pierce's sixteenth birthday party," she said, holding up the invitation.

"Really?" I was already making my way to the closets to change into something similar to her lavender silk mini.

"Yeah and she's having guests over from the Meeda tribe." We stared at each other. We both knew Noonie and Motif had made plans for Boaz to marry Noonie's niece, Neisha.

"Well, I guess Carmen and Shyamae will make their big introduction."

"Do you think they're ready?"

I looked at her as if she asked the most absurd question I've ever heard.

When it came to Boaz everything had to be planned ahead of time. When he was training for his black belt in Judo, he'd text his future mate every move he made *and* his opponent's too. Hell, he even trained with her on summer vacations to her homeland.

"They're more than ready."

We went to dinner with me dressed in white silk loose fitting pants with lavender trimming. I wore the matching robe with my hair down. We both had too many passionate marks for ponytails. Boaz and Pierce had the pleasure of introducing their mates to the rest of the pack at dinner.

The pack mates had their own dining hall in this wing. I had locks put on the outer wing doors, so the girls could roam freely without having to kill the many perverts that gawk at them. Like my father. Only my pack members have keys.

We started to talk amongst ourselves after prayer.

"Did you get your invitation," Karden asked, as always to my right and Jameria to my left and my brother to her left.

"Yeah. How did you know? Jameria said that Noonie came to her window."

"An invite was taped to my sitting room door when I went to change," he said, taking a bite of his salad.

Jameria had whole strawberries and sliced peaches as usual for her dinner. Her juices tasted just like that shit too. I picked up my spoon to taste the beef stew instead of Jameria.

"We're not staying long. It seems Noonie wants to see us."

He smiled. "The usual complaints?"

"The usual."

The conversation had turned in the direction of the newcomers gifts. Jameria and I made our excuse and went to see Noonie.

147

As usual she was on the phone in her sitting room with Motif on the tacky suede purple couch next to her. As soon as she hung up, she started on the bullshit.

"You two don't have to wait to be seated. I told you that we're family and that we should start acting like it more."

Damn it! I hate meeting with them.

Noonie was staring at me like a starving man about to attack his last meal, and a picture couldn't have done a better job if Motif was the painter. His eyes trailed every curve my mate's body have. I knew exactly when his exploration made it to her breast.

"That's okay, we're not staying," I said pulling Jameria up close to me.

That only made his eyes bulge when he saw the outline of her ass from the side in the mini. White high heeled sandals with tied up her calves made her long legs look even sexier than what they already were. He was now staring at the bite mark I made just above the back of her knee. His eyes landed on mine and I narrowed them.

"Tatum, that isn't fair. You never let your mate or your brother spend any time with us. We have every right to be a part of your lives as well as the rest of the pack." She narrowed her eyes at me. "You know you're not an adult yet, but you let your whole pack take summer vacations, taking Boaz and Pierce around the world without even talking with us, and we're his parents. Hell, you could at least invite us!" she said looking offended.

"You're *not* his mother. And you know as one of the future leaders, Boaz has to learn the world."

"Tatum, how many times have I told you not to talk to your stepmother like that?" Motif said, smiling at Jameria lusciously.

She narrowed her eyes at him and tightened her embrace around my waist. I tucked her closer under my left arm. Her five nine frame in heels was still a few inches shorter than my six five height.

Noonie rolled her eyes not caring if Motif is interested in other women. "Whatever. Anyway, I wanted to warn you and your mate that I want no shenanigans out of the two of you tomorrow at Pierce's party. His father has given me permission to host the event for his son's last chance at being a boy. It's not like you give them freedom or anything. Even on those little vacations, they have to work," she said shaking her head. "Anyway, we're having special guest tomorrow, so could you and your pack control your…mates?"

Jameria heard the hatred in her voice and smiled. "Noonie, you have nothing to worry about. We will be on our best behavior. We'll even help setup for the party."

Noonie looked at her suspiciously. "Why do you want to help me? Whenever you and the other young mates go shopping, you never ask me. Why offer a hand now?"

"If we'd known you were serious about going with us, we would've invited you. We just thought you were comfortable with your older friends."

She knew Noonie didn't have no damn friends. The only people she talked to on the phone was people she'd fucked, so Motif could get his land.

Jameria kept her expression sincere. Noonie accepted, then my baby went for the kill.

"Hey do you want to go to the mainland with the girls tomorrow? Cougar didn't go on the last trip with us, so Tyvine is allowing her a little freedom close to home."

Everyone on the island knew Tyvine *had* to keep Cougar on a short leash. That story would work without even trying.

"Sure. I'd love to go," she said, her expression lighting.

"If that will be all, then—"

"Hold on a second Tatum," Motif said standing. "Your eighteenth birthday is coming up. Jameria's in two months. Council wants to meet with you after you've returned from your hunt."

Okay, he's up to something. That's months away. Why is he bringing it up now? "About what?"

"To see if your mind changed about marriage to your mate. Don't get me wrong, I know you think you love each other, but you are both smart kids and probably have things in your life you want to accomplish before you wed... Then there's the possibility that something may happen to your mate to dishonor you someday."

I knew exactly what his bitch ass was up to. The problem was, so did Jameria.

We were fifteen at the time, uncle Demarcus told us about the time Motif and his Pack, were rumored to have done a gang rape on a pack member's mate to have her dishonored and banished from the island. I remember hearing Jameria say that if that ever happens to her, they wouldn't have to banish her. She'd happily leave after killing every asshole involved.

"Thanks for the warning," I said, grabbing Jameria's hand and storming out of the room before I jumped the gun and paralyzing his ass now.

She yanked me to a stop right outside of the north wing doors.

"Did you hear him...? You know what he's planning to do."

I went straight to the bedroom, toeing her behind me, locking the door. Too much shit has been on my mind lately but there's one I know I don't have to think about.

The agreement was that if a pack mate gives birth before her eighteenth birthday, then she's dishonored from the pack. I'll be eighteen in two months and Jameria two months later. The birthing ritual no longer scared me. I know she can take it. But I also know she won't agree to it, because she hasn't agreed to be my wife yet. And I can't take a chance like that. Jameria laid it all on the line in the beginning. She has goals she wants to accomplish before she marries. I can tell by the look in her eyes every time Rubea talks of her many adventures. And even though she loves me, I really can't say she won't leave me. When she walked away from her grandmother, she cried, but she walked. When she had to let Coral go... She cried, but she walked. And that was the worst. No, I can't take that chance. The only way to keep Jameria in my life is to knock her up, which will probably give her a good reason to kill me. But that's still cool too, because I'd rather be dead than to see her walk away.

"Don't worry about my father." Maybe if I explained it to my advantage, then she might agree. "He can't touch you if you're already pregnant," I said grabbing her around her waist. She'd stepped out of her mini and was headed to the shower.

"What the hell do you mean, 'if I was pregnant?'" she said with her fist propped on her curvy hips.

Shit!

"Nothing. I was just thinking, I'll be eighteen before we hunt and Motif won't be able to touch you if you're pregnant. And if you're worried about the birthing ritual...."

"Tatum," she said looking at me as if I was lost. "I'm seventeen years old-"

"Yeah, but you'll still be pregnant when you turn eighteen. You probably won't be showing by the time we marry."

At this she was surprised. "Tatum, I think you're jumping the gun here. I'm not going to have your baby and marry you just to keep Motif and his pack of hounds away from me," she said going into the bathroom.

I followed slowly, leaning against the counter. "That's not the only reason," I said quietly.

"I do love you, Jameria, and I want you to be with me. If *you* love me, you'll do this!"

Where the hell did that come from?

Jameria stared at me like I lost my damn mind. I think I did.

"You've never given me an ultimatum a day in my life." She turned her back on me and got in the shower.

I took a few deep breaths before undressing to join her. She had her head under the water.

I pulled her back into me.

"I'm sorry, I got carried away. I know you can take care of yourself. But to be on the safe side, how about you and the girls start your own garden. I'll have it fenced in with locks of your own." Part of the story about the gang rape was an injection of a drug substance in the girl's food or drink.

"I don't care Tatum. We'll start a garden if you think its best. But I will *not* have a baby until I'm ready, and nobody is going to make me."

I didn't say anything. If there was one thing I knew about Jameria, she was just as good at plotting shit as I could. *Since she won't agree to have my baby, then I will make her have it.*

Chapter Eighteen

It took a week to make the fertility pills look like birth control. My plan was to switch out the pills while she slept, but that would have been disastrous. She slept lightly, and knew every trick of the trade.

I couldn't ask Rubea to let me deliver them to her. Jameria would have known what was up and had the damn things destroyed. And I couldn't involve Karden, because she would have expected that. *No, I'll have to get someone who's closer to their mate than Kelanie.*

Her loyalty to Jameria would've been hazardous.

So I asked Moham to pick up the prescription from uncle Demarcus. Yesterday, I surprised him and Rubea with an all-expense paid trip to Germany, to get them away from Jameria. She would definitely have questions.

I told him to bring them straight to my room where I switched out Jameria's birth control for the vitamins. Then I told him to give them to Tyce so she could deliver them and not to mention that he stopped by my chambers first. He looked at me confused, but didn't say anything. Just shrugged his shoulders and went to do my bidding.

I didn't touch Jameria for almost three weeks. Whenever she asked about it, my excuse was that I wanted to be ready for the hunt and tournament. Then two weeks after her cycle and a week before we were due to leave for our hunt, I made my move and she was more than ready.

Motif was in the library court yards with a few of the wives of diplomatic husbands. I was supposed to meet Jameria here, but it was obvious she changed her mind. But then I saw her coming out of the library with an arm load of books.

She spotted my father and handed me her books, shaking her head. "One of these days, he's going to go after the wrong woman."

"As long as it's not mine," I said, kissing her lips before we started walking to her suite.

"I'm surprised you're not training for the hunt next week. You would normally train harder with it being so close."

Damn, she never missed a thing.

"Well, I've been neglecting you. It's way past time for making up." I said pulling her close to my side.

We were almost at the north wing, when I told her to, 'wait here'. I went to her bedroom, dropped the books on the desk and grabbed the big black bear skinned throw I had made for her from one of the packs hunts as a gift. She was puzzled when she saw what I had.

"Come on. Let's go to our spot." We took the trail through the forest to the waterfall.

Behind the gallons of water that was pouring down, a cave was hidden in the rocks. Jameria and I discovered it one day during our training. We only came here when we wanted to be away from the world. Not even my pack knows about this place. I'm not the type to keep too many secrets from them, but lately they seemed to be piling up on me. If they had any clue what I was about to do to their Mistress, they'd probably have me hog tied.

"We really didn't have to go out this far Tatum. We could've just told a pack member that we didn't want to be disturbed," she said leaning her head on my shoulder.

I smiled down at her but didn't say anything. A lot has been on my mind since I decided to go through with this. Like what will my pack think, my brother...Jameria. Will she *kill* me? Probably, but I'm not worried about dying. I'm more worried about her hating me. That, I will not be able to bare. To lose Jameria is not acceptable. She once told me, "If you really love someone or something, the greatest lesson learned is letting go. To have someone else's life under lock and key is slavery."

I hated that she thought of it that way, but it also gave me reason of *not* taking a chance to see what she'd do next at eighteen. Jameria was something like a snake. She liked to roam the earth and see different things. Marriage was definitely not at the top of her list.

I helped her take off her sandals so she could move along the rocks. A while back, we brought a sleeping bag, fire wood, candles and matches to our little hide out. She opened the slipping bag and spread the bear skinned throw on top while I lit a few candles in the dark cave. The waterfall made it chilly, so I decided to start a fire. Jameria got undressed and folded the throw over her. I stood, undressed and let my hair down before releasing her ponytail as well. She spread the throw wide with her legs up and open with it. She smiled at me with each foot touching the cave's walls. Damn, my baby was flexible. She knew exactly what I like.

Her hairless pussy smiled back at me sideways, drooling of that sweet nectar that I was craving to taste. I could've sworn I heard it say, 'long time, no see.' And just like before, I could smell her. The scent was deep and rich, like strawberry syrup. My pack and I talked about the animal instinct we all seem to be experiencing with our mates. It really didn't bother the women since they were already in tune with their animal side, but the guys and I thought we were going to lose our minds one night during a full moon. We all must have come at the same time because I heard every pack member (except Boaz and Pierce, thank God) howls in the north wing that night.

Now her heat was calling to me once again. I moved toward her slowly to pace myself.

She looked annoyed and impatient, then lean forward, taking my face between her hands, shoving her tongue in my mouth. Damn. It tasted just like peaches.

She pushed me on my back and climbed on top, easing down on my length and stopping on occasion to give her tight wet pussy a few squeezes to accommodate my size. My baby, never the type to beat around the bush. She grind her pelvic bone against mine while rotating her ass and squeezing her pussy muscles on my dick. I watched as each of her abdomen muscles move up and down in wave's unison to her pussy. Then she

157

began to move up and down and her walls got tighter, wetter.

Damn!!!

I wanted to explode. I reached behind her and held my left ball and began messaging her clit with my right thumb in a circular motion. She moaned, and began bouncing on my dick like a pogo stick. She was about to climax. I let go of myself and grabbed her hips bringing her down harder.

"Cum with me baby," I said looking up at her. She grinded her clit against my thumb and rolled her muscles up along my shaft, suctioning every drop of my sperm from my balls.

Exactly what I wanted. And I was nowhere near tired. I came in Jameria at least six times before I turned her over and began pounding in her ass.

For the rest of the week, I'd been fucking her all over the palace, taking every opportunity to plant my seeds in her. I even fucked her in the Council Hall bathroom during one of their meetings. Her ass was pent against the bathroom wall before they began prayer.

The day before we were due to leave was supposed to be the first day of her cycle. It didn't make it, so I treated myself to another round of sweet flowing juices. I ate her pussy out that whole night. She was worried that her period was going to come down with one of her climaxes. But *I* wasn't worried. I was happy knowing that my seed might be growing inside her. (Without her knowledge, of course). It was too soon to tell, but I knew he or she was in there. I didn't even enter her vagina that night for fear I might hurt it. One of the disadvantages of having a long dick. Scared you might take the life of something you really want. If that's possible. I was eighteen now and Jameria will be eighteen by the time I return. *I hope she doesn't destroy the life that might be growing inside of her.*

The next day, we stood at the edge of the forest with the rest of the pack and their mates saying our goodbyes. Jameria and the girls snuck the two younger mates out to say their goodbyes to Boaz and Pierce. (Noonie was unable to have her party due to a hurricane.) We watched as Boaz's tongue slipped in and out of his mate's mouth like one of Jameria's snakes. I'll have to have a talk with his ass on this hunt. The boy was out of control.

I turned my attention back to Jameria and pulled her close up to me, placing my forehead on hers. "You know I'm going to miss you the whole time I'm away," I said, kissing her soft plump lips.

"I'll miss you, too. I don't know how I'll be able to get through training without you."

I immediately thought of the baby that might be growing inside of her. "Sweetie, try not to overdo it with your training. I don't want you to hurt yourself."

She looked at me puzzled. "How is that possible?"

I tried to play off my panic by taking her hand and leading her away from the rest of the group. "Sweetheart, I just don't want you to overdo it and end up with biceps like mine," I said cupping her face between my hands. "If I come home looking for my curvy body and end up finding a third leg, I'll be highly pissed."

She smiled and kissed the palm of my hand. "In that case, I'll be extra careful," she said throwing her arms around my neck for a heart stopping, tongue twisting kiss. We walked back to the group and I kissed her one last time before leaving with my pack. By the time we return, Jameria should be at least two to three months pregnant with my child. I pray the love I see in her eyes now, will be there when I return.

Karden stopped me halfway through the woods. "What's on your mind Tatum?"

I stared at him. "What makes you think something is on my mind?"

"Come on, Tatum," he said grinning. "I've been your best friend before I could walk. It's not hard for me to tell when something is bothering you."

It was on the tip of my tongue to tell him the truth. But every time I thought about what I'd done to Jameria, I felt lower than Motif looks.

Chapter Nineteen

The past two months felt longer than any other hunt we've ever been on. I guess it's because I was anxious to see my mate. That's if I still have one. Not a day went by that I didn't have Jameria on my mind. She turned eighteen four days ago. I wish I'd been there to welcome her to adulthood, but if she received her checkup this month, then she already got my gift.

"Man, I can't wait to get home. I think I'm going to sit in the tub for at least two hours," Cole said. He was helping Moham carry the huge dead boar on a spear we'd rigged up.

"Well, I can't wait for Jameria to formally become my sister," Boaz said grinning from ear to ear. "So, are you proposing to her as soon as we get back?"

Everyone turned for my reply. "I think you're jumping the gun Boaz. I don't know if that is what she wants." They all looked at me confused, but I would not give them any more info.

As we exit the woods into the palace court yard, we could see the mates walking toward us rapidly.

"That's what I'm talking about," Moham said. "An instant welcome home."

I noticed Jameria wasn't in the bunch and the closer the girls got, the harder their expressions became. Then I saw her. She was standing in the center of the courtyard, but her posture wasn't welcoming. It was aggressive.

The girls had made it to us and crouched defensively in front of their mates.

"What the hell is going on?" Karden asked.

I didn't need an explanation. I knew without asking, 'Why is there a defensive line against their Mistress?' Shit, who could look at her face and not tell that she is pissed. And she didn't waste no time trying to get to my ass.

She'd flipped high in the air with custom made jeans on to magnify every sensual curve as she landed inches in front of Cougar and Tyvine. Cougar opened her mouth to call her cats, but Jameria already had her hand around the poor girl's throat. When it came to strategy, Jameria was the best at it. It's common sense to take out your strongest opponent first.

Tyvine didn't know what to do.

Kelanie opened her mouth to call to her birds, but Jameria had hauled Cougar's struggling body into Kelanie's, knocking the wind out if her. Jameria stared right at me. Nothing was going to stop her from getting what she wanted. And the only thing I saw in her eyes was blood. She wanted my blood.

Boaz, Pierce, Cole, and Karden, jumped forward wrapping their arms around her as restraints.

"Mistress, please stop! What are you doing?" Karden was looking from me to her, wondering why she was trying to attack me and why I was doing nothing to stop her.

"Take your hands off my mate, please," I said firm, but calmly.

As soon as they released her, she jumped high, landing on my shoulders, wrapping her soft muscular thighs around my neck. Before I fell backwards, I saw Motif and his retired pack coming toward us. Moham crouched over Tyce after hearing her bear ramble. They were at the center point of our group with two humongous black bears on each side of them.

I finally managed to wrestle my way from Jameria's grip to see Motif stop his advance. I barked out 'The Pack Call' and the rest of my pack and mates, joined Moham and Tyce, blocking Jameria and me from his view. I rolled over and climbed on top, holding her arms and legs down, using my body weight. I hate to have to do this. Especially if she's pregnant, or if she ever was. She wasn't trying to smother me with her thighs for nothing.

"Can you hold off from killing me, until we're alone," I whispered in her ear. Probably taking in her brown sugar and strawberry scent for the last time.

She didn't answer, so I sat up a little to look in her eyes.

Damn! If looks could kill, I would've been dead yesterday, just from the thought.

"Be in my suite in five minutes and don't make me wait." She stood and walked between both groups without even the hint of an explanation for her actions.

I didn't bother giving an answer myself. Just followed her to her suite with both groups even more confused and puzzled. I told my group as I passed to go to their own chambers and to take their mates with them. The last thing I need was casualties for this fight. *Maybe, if I lock her in the north wing, I might be the only one dying.*

I locked every door behind me as I entered. She was in her sitting room, waiting in her black-on-black high-back chair. A hot shower first is definitely out of the question for right now. I dropped my duffel bag on the floor by the door and then made my way to my own high-back chair, opposite hers.

We stared each other down before she spoke. "You don't seem surprised I tried to kill you. After your explanation, I'll finish what I started," she said, crossing her legs. "And make sure you speak the truth, because I had the birth control tested."

Shit!

I didn't hold anything back. She stood, pacing the floor as I spoke.

"I wouldn't have done this, if you'd just agree to be my wife. Hell, I don't see what the big deal is anyway. We've been sleeping together for the past six years. It would be only natural for you to birth my child."

"Tatum, I told you this is something that I did *not* want right now. You either for that matter."

I turned and looked at her. "I think we're ready. I know we will survive the ritual."

"You asshole," she said, shaking her head at me. "After I have this baby, I'm leaving. You, being more concerned about getting what you want, didn't even think about the fact that I would still be going through pain. Not you! Fuck you and that ritual." She went in her bedroom and I followed.

"Jameria, I know I've hurt you in the worst way possible, but please," I said dropping to my knees, locking my arms around her still small waist. "Don't leave me. You can still have your freedom and travel the world, but please, please, don't take the only means of me being happy."

"Don't worry Tatum," she said, placing a hand atop of my head. "I'm leaving. You can keep your child." She eased out of my embrace and went to start her shower.

I slowly followed, getting undressed on my way. "Jameria," I said stepping in behind her. "I love you so much. Please think about what you're saying."

"Tatum, were you thinking about me or yourself when you decided to switch my birth control for fertility pills?"

I didn't even bother answering.

"Just as I thought. The only person on your mind is you. Well, that's cool too. I don't need you to care about my needs. I can take care of myself."

"How can you say that? You know I care about you—"

"Did you tell any of your pack brothers what you've done?"

"No. I imagine their mates are telling them now."

"Why would they do that? They didn't plot to get me pregnant. You did. Besides, I didn't want to be the one to tell them their so called *Chief* deceived me."

165

"Jameria, can't you see that I did it out of love? Just thinking about you walking away, nearly killed me. I'm not the type to go around taking whatever I want and I'm hurting now because you think so little of me."

She turned and faced me. "Tatum stop and think about what you've done. Then think about what we *still* have to do."

I did as she asked and the first thing popped in my head was Boaz. Shit!

"Boaz hasn't made sixteen yet," I said in a low voice.

"And?"

"And what?"

"The tournament. How long do you think you and The Pack will be able to hold off your urges? Not understanding your animal side that's hanging by a thin thread or afraid on the next full moon, one of you might fuck one of us to death. We won't be able to enter the tournament now." She grasped my shoulders, like she wanted to shake some commonsense into me. "We'll have to wait another three years. I can't be around the snakes until the baby is born. We have to introduce Shyamae' and Carmen to the Council *after* Boaz's birthday and…" She had that attack mode on her face again. "Since you were so anxious for a baby, I have to inform Council of my pregnancy." She held up her hand before I started to protest. "I know they can't make me leave, but I'm *not* going to marry you Tatum. If you'd just trusted what we had, then you would know when I spoke of my future, you was already there. But the problem was you didn't want to wait. We could've stayed on a college campus this year, getting our masters. We could've had months at a time away from Noonie, your father, Council, and responsibilities. But what the fuck did you do? Instead of taking some of our burdens away, you decided to add on."

By this time the tears were streaming down her beautiful, bronze face.

What have I done? What the fuck have I done? She's right. We could have waited until we were twenty-one. I could have been beside her on epic journeys around the world. I jumped the gun. Instead of keeping her close to me, I was driving her away.

Jameria grabbed a big towel, stepping out of the shower. For the first time, she didn't wash my back and I didn't wash hers. I stepped out of the shower, not even bothering to dry off, and went into the closet. She was pulling out a black satin mini dress with ties around the neck. I took the dress out of her hand and pulled her close to my chest, hugging her with fierceness.

"Jameria, you're right. I'm so sorry. I never intended to trap you. Since you're not marrying me, you don't have to go through with the ritual. The only thing I ask is, if you could please find it in your heart to forgive me. I still need you as my best friend and if I can't have you as that either, then please just don't leave hating me."

She pressed her lips to my neck. "I don't hate you Tatum. Just disappointed."

I don't know why, but the word 'disappointed' made me feel worse. We met up with the pack and their mates at dinner, and I told them everything I'd done. It was hard not to show emotion when you know you've fucked up. But that's also why I want Jameria as my wife. Even though I hurt her beyond repair, she still stood by my side as a devoted mate and came to my rescue at the first sign of a breakdown.

"This only means Tatum will be Island Chief much sooner," she said looking at each and every member. "It's true we won't be able to participate in the tournament, but it also gives us time to concentrate on our other goals."

Boaz raised his hand. I guess it was impossible to avoid questions at this time. "What is it Boaz?"

"Why do you have to tell Council now? Why don't you just get married and tell them afterwards?"

Damn it! The one question I was hoping to avoid.

"Bo-"

"We're still discussing that," Jameria said before I had the chance to fuck something else up.

"Just don't take too long," Cole said smiling. "We don't want to have to explain to Council why you're walking down the aisle with a basketball under your dress."

"No wonder you tried to kill him," Moham said, laughing.

Everyone around the table was laughing and having a good time with the events of the day. But what if they knew the truth of her planning to leave. She bought us some time for now, but what about later, when they find out there won't be a wedding.

I went to my chambers after dinner to shower and take a nap, praying Jameria would accept my offer and spend the night with me. I would've stayed at her place but I wanted the choice to be hers if she wanted me or not. Like that shit was going to make a difference.

Later on that night, I heard my bedroom door open, then close. Thank you, God! She decided to come. I reached out to her silhouette from the moonlight and pulled her on top of me.

"I thought you weren't going to come."

Then the scent hit me.

It wasn't her brown sugar. And her smooth skin felt dry. I reached over and switched on the lamp to find Noonie sitting on my dick. I shoved her ass on the floor and stood up.

Just then Jameria came into the room and flipped the light switch on.

"What the hell are you doing in here?"

She didn't give her time to answer. Jameria lunged forward and grabbed Noonie by her already thinning hair and dragged her ass into the sitting room, where she convene to whipping her ass. Noonie was screaming so loud everyone in the palace tried to crowd in here. Motif stepped forward to pull Jameria off but, changed his mind when I crouched in front of the ass whipping.

"Tatum, if you don't let me pull her off, she'll kill her!"

Karden and Tyvine walked past Motif and me and pulled Jameria up restraining her arms to her sides, sandwiching her between them. Cougar and Kelanie took my flanks, so I stood and backed up to take my mate from my brothers' arms.

"Are you alright?"

"Are you serious," Motif said, helping Mara pick his mate up off my floor. "She nearly kills your stepmother and you ask if she's okay? She should be exiled for this incident alone!"

"When your mate retrieves consciousness ask her why she was in my room. Until then, can you please get out and take her stank ass with you?"

Motif looked as if he wanted to jump forward, but Cougar was already there and waiting.

"He said leave…Unless you want to join your mate in her nap?" He stared at her, until Tyvine crouched down taking her flank.

"I see justice won't be done tonight." He turned to the people in the room. "I'll call a Council meeting tomorrow!" Then he turned back to me. "She could have killed her and you wouldn't have cared one bit!"

"Look at what your mate have on and where she was tonight, *then* you can tell me how wrong we are for our actions."

Motif looked down at the red satin panty and bra set his mate wore, then stormed out.

"We'll still call a Council meeting tomorrow, Tatum." I didn't know my uncle Demarcus had entered the room. "Noonie had no right being in here. It's time we did something about that. You guys go get some sleep. I'll see all of you bright and early in the morning."

Once everyone was gone, I closed my sitting room door and locked my bedroom door.

Jameria was lying in the bed on her side. "I saw her peeping through your bedroom window, so I decided to wait and a little while to see what she was going to do next."

"I guess she was trying to make sure the coast was clear." I laid down facing her. "I thought it was you, until I caught the scent and switched the lamp on."

"I thought as much." She gazed at me, then very slowly put a soft hand against my cheek.

"I'm mad as *hell* at you... but I cannot handle you being with someone else, even if they tried to force themselves on you."

My hand was against her still muscular abdomen, and before I knew it the words flowed from my tongue. "Jameria, my plan was never to take your freedom and until you explained it to me earlier, I realized that I'm truly fucked up. I panicked because I thought you were going to leave me if Motif tried anything or just not having you at my side. But I can't deny how happy I am that you're carrying my child. And we don't have to get married if that's what you want. We'll think of some—,"

She placed her hand over my mouth. "I do want to marry you, just not this soon," she whispered. "I wanted us to at least experience a couple of years traveling and college life. Tatum, we never really had the chance to be young. We've had responsibilities since the day we met. But I always knew you were going to be my husband."

I'd better not get my hopes up, but they sure as hell was climbing the ladder. "Are you saying that you'll marry me?"

CPSIA information can be obtained
at www.ICGtesting.com
Printed in the USA
LVHW041623301022
731931LV00007B/313

9 781788 231831